The
Adventures
of a
South Pole
Pig

The
Adventures of a
South Pole Pig
A novel of
Chris Kurtz

The Adventures of a South Pole Pig

Chris Kurtz

Illustrations by
Jennifer Black Reinhardt

HOUGHTON MIFFLIN HARCOURT

Boston   New York

For information about permission to reproduce selections from this book, write to
trade.permissions@hmco.com or to Permissions, Houghton Mifflin Harcourt
Publishing Company, 3 Park Avenue, 19th Floor, New York, New York 10016.

www.hmhco.com

The text of this book is set in Garamond 3 LT Std.
The illustrations are done in black ink.

The Library of Congress has cataloged the hardcover edition as follows:
Kurtz, Chris, 1960–
The adventures of a South Pole pig : a novel of snow and courage / Chris Kurtz ;
illustrations by Jennifer Black Reinhardt.
p. cm.
Summary: "Flora the pig ditches the sedentary life on the farm
for an adventure in Antarctica, where she escapes the knife and lives her dream
of pulling a sled with a team of dogs."—Provided by publisher.
[1. Pigs—Fiction. 2. Adventure and adventurers—Fiction.
3. Dogsledding—Fiction. 4. Sled dogs—Fiction. 5. Dogs—Fiction.
6. Antarctica—Fiction.]
I. Reinhardt, Jennifer Black, 1963– illustrator. II. Title.
PZ7.K9626Ad 2012
[Fic]—dc23
2012027226

ISBN: 978-0-547-63455-5 hardcover
ISBN: 978-0-544-54070-5 paperback

Printed in the United States of America
DOC 20 19 18 17
4500786966

✳

For Carolyn,

My North Star —C.K.

Chapter 1

"Mama, why do we have to live in a cage?" Flora dug in the dirt at something hard and rusty.

"Honey, don't do that." Her mother nosed her away. "And it's not a cage. It's a pigpen."

"Same thing," said Flora under her breath.

How unlucky she was—born with adventurous hooves that were stuck inside a pen. But she wasn't giving up. If there was a way out, Flora said to herself, she would find it.

She had already packed down trails to each corner of the pen. She had poked her wet snout through every wooden slat to smell the other side. And she had dug holes all along the pen's perimeter. Usually the only thing hiding under the surface was more dirt—until today. Maybe this hard and rusty something would bring a change in routine.

As soon as her mother turned, Flora went back to digging. She scratched away busily until the thing popped out of the ground.

"I knew it." Flora gave a little squeal of joy. Now she had to see what it could do.

"Flora!" shouted her mother.

Flora took a step back.

Her mother trotted over, and close on her heels were three brothers. Flora had seven, so there was always at least one around to watch her get into trouble.

"Rusty pieces of metal are very dangerous. Why do you insist on unearthing things better left alone?" said her mother.

Flora stamped the ground. "If it's unexplored then it needs to get dug up."

"I see," said Mother. "Well if it is sharp and rusty, then it needs to stay unexplored and underground." Her mother used her snout to nudge and scoot the nail over to the wooden fence, where there was a space between the ground and the lowest board.

"Mama, wait! I'm not done with that thingy yet." Flora shoved herself between her mother's legs.

Her mother pushed her back. "You most certainly *are* done with this thingy, little one." With a firm kick, she spun the nail under the board and out of sight.

Flora screwed up her face, not sure if she should stomp or flop on the ground. But before she could choose, her mother lay down with her back against the fence. "Breakfast time!" she called.

A thrill ran through Flora. She was hungry.

So were her brothers.

Flora dove for a good spot, only to find herself bumped and turned aside.

"There's enough for everyone," Mother said. Nobody listened.

But Flora, the firstborn of the litter, had sturdy shoulders and strong back legs. When she failed to push through, she had other ways to make room for herself. Standing on a brother's ear usually created an opening. And if that didn't work, she'd use her sharp teeth. Flora found that if she chomped down on a brother's tail, she could count on a loud squeal and an open space.

A girl had to fight for her food in this family—except against little Alfred, the runt. If he started sniffling, Flora made room for two.

After breakfast was naptime. Little pigs with their tummies round and full of milk flopped against one another on the ground. But Flora thought piglets spent too much of their lives sleeping. Today she pawed her brother's knee. "Sam, wake up."

"Ummm," Sam grunted. He didn't move.

Flora went over to Tommy. His ear was flopped open.

"Boo." Tommy's head snapped up. "Naptime's over," she said.

"Go away." Tommy laid his head back down and folded his ear closed.

Flora returned to Sam. She thought about standing on his tail.

Just behind her someone else grunted. When Flora turned, she saw Alfred smiling and twitching in his sleep.

"Alfred!" She walked over to her littlest brother, who opened his eyes. "It's time to go exploring."

"Flora, I have a full tummy, and that always makes me sleepy. Besides, we explored the whole pen yesterday, and there wasn't one new, exciting thing."

"What about that nail I just dug up?"

Alfred closed his eyes. "New, but not exciting."

"Fine." Flora turned her back. She had to admit he was right. But if anything exciting ever did pop up, she'd be the first to see it, if she kept exploring.

She trotted over to the manure pile, Flora's favorite lookout. It was the highest point in the pigpen and the only place Flora could hope to see anything interesting beyond her small world. She gazed past the shade of the pigpen roof to where the world was bright and sunny—sunny junk heap, sunny grass, sunny cornfield, sunny gravel road. A familiar sound floated in. Flora cocked her head to one side to listen. Dogs. They were barking again.

Now, seeing a dog would be exciting! What would it look like? she wondered. Woolly like a sheep? Horned like a bull? Single-hoofed like a horse or double-hoofed like a pig? One thing was sure, dogs made more noise than all of the other animals put together.

As the barking died down, Flora tilted her head up at the pigpen roof. Sunlight poured through little holes, showing bits of dust in the air. Flora moved so that one point of light landed on her front leg. This was as much direct sun as Flora ever got. She lay down carefully so that the spot of light stayed on her leg, and she watched it.

It looked like a little star. Mother had told her about the points of light that came out at night, like a hundred eyes, watching and twinkling high above the world. Flora wished she could see those eyes.

When the spot of light moved off her leg, she scrambled up and this time looked all around.

Behind her was an empty pigpen. To her right was the open side of the barn. Flora could see through it to the three horse stalls on the far wall. Only one had housed a horse for the last three days. Nessie was quiet except when her hooves knocked against the wooden walls.

Flora turned back to the sunshine and the junk heap.

There were old tires, machine parts, wavy rafts of chicken wire, and broken tools that lay where they had been tossed. In the middle was a wheelbarrow with no wheel, and in its body was a green garden hose coiled around . . .

A white fur ball?

Flora looked again. Was that a dog? The fur ball stretched and yawned. It had a black ear and a mouth full of sharp teeth. Flora's front knees trembled. This was new and exciting!

The creature stepped down from the wheelbarrow and walked carelessly toward the pigpen. Should Flora warn her mother? No. She could handle the intruder.

She crept off the manure pile and pushed herself close to the fence where the fur ball might enter, if it was foolish enough to step inside a pigpen guarded by a fierce, sharp-hoofed piglet. She hadn't woken up today expecting a fight, but this was going to be very satisfying. If some prowling food thief thought it could sneak into her home, Flora was just the pig to teach it a lesson. She crouched.

Sure enough, the fur ball slipped like water through the slats in the fence.

This was it, the moment Flora would leap and . . .

The fur ball sat down and began to lick itself.

Flora managed to stop from pouncing to watch. Its little pink tongue went in and out of its toothy mouth, licking the fur in front and then working from one side to the other.

This was perfect. It was so busy, it would never see her coming. Flora gathered herself and then launched.

"Hiyaaaaaaa!" she squealed.

Chapter 2

The stranger didn't twirl around or scream in fear. Instead, it flew to the top of a fence post in one motion, as easily as if it were a bird, and sat blinking.

Flora slid to a stop and put her front feet up on the post. "Did I scare you?"

"Terrified." The furry white creature gave itself another lick.

"I've got rock-hard hooves and a mouthful of sharp teeth." Flora opened her mouth to show how sharp they were. "You'd better be careful."

"Such terrible weapons. I'm lucky I'm still alive."

"My name is Flora, and I'm a pig," said Flora. "I'm in charge around here and . . ." She stopped because the animal had turned its head to lick its back. Flora wasn't sure it was listening.

"And I like your fur because it's all white like mine." Flora didn't know why she had said this to an animal that might be an enemy. "Are you a dog?"

"My name is Luna, and I am most certainly *not* a dog. I'm a cat, and I like your spirit," she said.

"We could be sisters," said Flora.

Luna gazed at Flora for a moment. "We're not sisters." She went back to her licking.

Flora walked to the other side of the post to get a different view. "Why do you keep doing that?"

"Doing what?"

"Licking yourself."

"It's how I keep clean."

Flora stuck out her tongue and gave her shoulder a lick. It tickled her tongue in a way that didn't feel very good, and, besides, it tasted funny.

"I don't lick myself," Flora announced, and

rubbed her tongue on the top of her mouth to get rid of the tickly feeling.

"I can tell," said Luna. "And that is why we're not sisters."

A soft breeze made Luna's fur move like a wave. "Can I feel your fur?" Flora asked.

Luna hopped down. "Now, that's a request a cat can never refuse." She rubbed her white fur along Flora's side, and her tail slipped under Flora's neck.

Flora had never felt anything so soft—not even Mother's underbelly or Alfred's silky ears.

Luna walked over to the fence and turned. "I hope you don't mind if I come back to visit someday even if we're not sisters. I'll try to remember to stay away from those rock-hard hooves of yours."

Flora's heart lurched. "You're going already?"

Luna looked surprised. "I'm a cat. I come and go as I please." She slid between the boards and disappeared.

A squeal slipped out. Flora couldn't help it. She wasn't proud of such a piggy noise. But *she* wanted so much to be able to come and go as she pleased. And her best chance for adventure of the whole day—the whole week and even the whole month—was leaving.

"Hey, relax." One of Luna's eyes appeared in the crack.

Flora made her voice behave. "Take me with you."

"You're not a cat—you're a pig, remember? I

wander around and see things, and you . . . you stay in this pigpen and . . . do pig stuff."

"But I don't want to do pig stuff," Flora whispered. "I want to wander around."

"Why?" Luna poked her head back inside the pen.

"I'm curious," said Flora.

"Hmm." Luna rubbed the side of her head against a board. "Curious. That's a good quality. It shows you have spirit. Though some think being curious means you're looking for trouble. I'll go do some wandering. Then I'll come back and tell you what I find. Stay out of trouble." She drew her head back through the crack.

"But I don't want to stay out of trouble!" Flora called. "I want something to happen around here!"

There was a silence, and then Luna's head poked through the fence once more. "Oh, it will. You don't have to look for trouble. It will find you. And when that happens"—Luna disappeared, but her voice continued—"keep up that great spirit and make a plan, because nine lives is just a state of mind."

What plan? Flora raced back to the top of the manure pile and watched until Luna's tall waving tail rounded the corner of the barn.

Flora sighed. With a heart born for adventure and hooves stuck in a pen, Flora couldn't help thinking that trouble might be a good thing.

Chapter 3

After breakfast the next day, Flora sat on top of the manure pile while her lazy brothers snored away again. Too bad for them—they wouldn't be making any new friends or learning new things or getting ready for trouble.

She stood up on her hind legs and waved her front hooves in the air. Luna would probably think that looked pretty spirited, if only she were here to watch. Luna. Luna. Flora put all her thoughts into wishing the cat back, and then . . .

There she was, slipping through the junk heap, her beautiful white flag of a tail following behind. Flora bundled down the manure pile to meet her.

"Hi, Luna!"

"Hi, Flora." Luna hopped on a fence post.

"Watch this!" Flora spun around in a dizzying circle. She dashed to the top of the manure pile, did a two-legged walk, then raced back down, barely managing to stop herself before banging her snout into the fence.

"Wow," said Luna.

"How's that for spirit?" Flora was breathing hard.

"I never knew pigs could have so much." Luna sounded as if she meant it. "You almost looked like a horse galloping up that manure pile."

"Like Nessie?" Flora put her small hooves up on the post and looked over at the large hooves peeking out from underneath the horse stall door.

"Nessie used to be the fastest thing on the farm, but she's older now and her front leg bothers her. Don't get on her bad side, because she can still kick when she gets grouchy. She hates being cooped up for too long."

That was exactly how Flora felt. She waited to hear more about grouchy Nessie, but Luna lifted her left hind foot and began licking between her toes.

"I've been getting ready for trouble," said Flora.

Luna stopped licking but didn't put her foot back where it was supposed to go. She looked at Flora as if she didn't understand.

Flora tried again. "You know, like you said, it always finds you."

"Oh, yeah." Luna sat up straight. "The trouble with trouble is it's a hard thing to prepare for. Speaking of trouble, this farm would be a great place to wander around, if it weren't crawling with dogs. Maybe you've heard them."

Flora nodded enthusiastically. "What do you know about dogs?"

"I know they howl just to hear themselves howl. I know if they get off their leash—and they always do—then look out, because no one is safe."

Flora felt a little thrill go through her. She would be happy to teach a dog a lesson. "Why is the farm crawling with dogs?"

"Training," said Luna. "The dogs on this farm are being trained for expeditions, which are the same things as adventures."

"Adventures?" Flora couldn't believe her ears. How could anyone be so lucky?

"It starts when they're puppies. About your age. First they get used to the lines and ropes and harnesses. Then comes the real work."

Trained for adventure. Flora couldn't get over it.

"They pull loads that get heavier and heavier," Luna said. "Dogs might be annoying, but on this farm, they are the hardest working animals of all."

"Why do they have to pull so——" Flora stopped.

Luna had slipped down to the ground, almost without moving a muscle. Now she was staring at the top of Flora's head in the strangest way. Flora shook her head in case she had a bit of manure stuck to one of her ears.

But Luna didn't stir except for her tail, which stuck straight out behind her and trembled at the tip. Then she lowered herself into a crouch, and her eyes got very wide. Flora realized they weren't fixed on her at all but on something behind her.

Flora turned slowly. The dirt beside the fence was moving. No, wait. It wasn't dirt. Flora peered closer. It was the same color as dirt but hairy. Then Flora saw a long, naked tail.

"Look out. It's a rat," Luna whispered.

Chapter 4

Trouble. Flora was delighted—but scared, too. The creature in the dirt fit Mother's description perfectly. Mother said rats were a terrible curse on any farm. They were dirty. They were thieves. But mostly they were meaner than a bad toothache. And she also said piglets should stay far away from them.

As Flora took a step sideways, she felt soft fur slide by her. Luna was creeping low to the ground toward the hay bale.

"Luna, don't go any closer," Flora whispered.

"Shhh." Luna brought another paw forward and put it down gently on the dirt. "Rats in the rigging," she murmured. "Time to tangle."

Luna flowed ahead one more cat length, gathered her back feet under herself, and then exploded

21

onto the rat. The rat shrieked and turned his teeth to meet his attacker.

"Luna!" Flora shouted. "Get away!"

But the fighters became a single white and brown ball bouncing off the fence. Dirt and fluffs of fur flew up around them. Flora's rump bumped against the fence on the other side. She hadn't even noticed that she was backing up.

The rat's long hose of a tail flailed against the ground, and for an instant he broke free. Then Luna was on him again. She seemed to have hooks and daggers. She was battle ready.

She pinned the shrieking rat on his belly. As he strained his head back to land a bite, Luna sank her teeth deep into his neck. He quivered, mouth open, and then lay still.

Luna did not release him at first. Her eyes blinked slowly, but her teeth stayed right where they were. The swirl of dirt and fur settled on Luna and all around. She gave the rat a shake and then ever so slowly released her grip. After taking a step back, she hopped up on a fence post and began to clean herself.

Flora looked away from the frightening scene—only to see Mother and a half circle of awestruck piglets watching too.

Mother came forward. "On behalf of myself and my family, thank you."

Luna stopped her cleaning. "Please don't mention it. We all have our tasks on the farm, and I am happy to do my part."

"It is very much appreciated," said Mother. "And now if you would be so kind, please remove this nasty, vile creature from our home."

"Naturally, madam."

Flora looked back at the rat. His open mouth showed long yellow teeth. His eyes were open too.

Jumping down from her perch, Luna stepped around the rat to find a good grip, then seized him in her teeth, and, moving backwards, began to drag him over the dirt. Flora was surprised at how big the rat was—as big as Luna's head. He was also clearly heavy, judging from the way Luna strained as she tugged.

Flora trotted forward to help.

"Flora!" Her mother's voice made her stop. "Not another step."

"I thought you said I should be helpful." Flora watched as Luna slowly eased herself through the slats in the fence. The rat disappeared one tiny jerk at a time.

"Flora, honey. Let the cat do what cats do. You just worry about what pigs do."

And what do pigs do? Flora wondered. She was afraid she knew the answer: Nothing.

As she drifted off to sleep that night, her mind filled with a determined thought—almost a plan. Maybe most pigs did nothing but eat and sleep. But that wasn't good enough for this pig. When trouble came next time, Flora would be ready.

Chapter 5

After breakfast, Flora gathered the piglets together to announce a new game. "It's called Cats and Rats."

"Yay!" her brothers cheered.

"Who wants to be a rat?"

The cheering stopped.

"Flora," came a warning.

Flora glanced around to see her mother rubbing her shoulder against a fence post. She wasn't looking at her children, but clearly she was paying attention.

Flora turned back to her brothers. "Good news, everyone," she said. "In this game, nobody has to be a rat."

Her brothers cheered again.

"Okay, all you cats." Flora's eyes swept the ground to either side of her. "We need to look for a rat substitute."

In a moment they had two suitable imitations. One was half an orange with all of the juice squeezed out. The other was a balled-up paper bag.

Flora decided to use the paper bag first and nosed it into the circle of piglets.

"Stand clear," she commanded, backing up a few steps and then crouching onto her belly. "Watch and learn—and when I give you the signal, say, 'Rats in the rigging—time to tangle.'"

Flora crept forward, making an effort to stay very low. This wasn't as easy as Luna made it look. Flora's legs dragged on the ground instead of stepping cleanly. But she managed to stay down.

"Now!" she said.

"Rats in the rigging—time to tangle," the piglets chanted.

Flora concentrated on making her tail twitch and hoped it was working even though she couldn't see. She drew a few steps closer. Then, gathering her legs under her, Flora sprang forward and leaped on the paper bag. It made a satisfyingly loud crunch as she stomped it into the ground with her hooves.

Her brothers cheered and then, under Flora's watchful eye, tried out their own rat-attack styles until the paper bag was a tattered mess that no longer crunched at all.

"All right," Flora announced. "Time for Rat Number Two."

Unbelievably, the others were already tired. As she watched, they flopped down against one another for their morning nap.

Well, she didn't need them to practice.

Flora crouched and attacked. The orange peel flipped up and rolled toward the fence. Flora charged again and missed. Her shoulder smacked into the lowest board.

Ow.

But wait. Was that a cracking sound she'd

heard? She looked around to make sure the piglets hadn't stirred. Mother was asleep too.

Flora leaned against the fence board again. It moved under her weight. She pressed forward. The board gave a soft wooden creak and then parted into two pieces. She slipped through until her head was free, then carefully and quietly crawled all the way out.

Flora looked around. She was standing near the junk heap! There was the broken wheelbarrow! There were the broken tools and chicken wire!

She had escaped the pigpen at last!

Chapter 6

Flora scampered past the junk heap and around the corner of the barn.

Bright sunshine made her blink. The green grass under her hooves felt springy and alive. The warmth on her back made her want to squeal and kick up her back legs. But she was pretty sure this would attract attention, maybe even a dog.

Flora quickly glanced around, but she was alone.

A gravel road led out from the barn, but where it went, Flora couldn't see. Off to one side of the road was a cornfield, and off to the other side was more green grass. There were fences all over, but none could keep her from going where she wanted to go. Without another thought, she trotted down the road, her hooves click-clicking on the gravel.

Was she still too loud? What happened to piglets that escaped and got caught? She didn't like thinking about that.

Flora wiggled under a fence into the cornfield. It was cool and quiet beneath the leaves. Only green light made it through to this secret place, and it filled her with energy. She dashed off between two rows of corn. She turned sharply and zigzagged between the stalks. Wheeeee! The tall plants shivered as she bumped them. With green flying by on either side, she zigzagged back the other way. The world of a cornfield seemed large and small at the same time. Flora could hardly see three feet in front of her; yet she knew that the field went on and on.

Flora plowed to a stop.

Why was she buzzing around in circles like a barnyard fly? Lucky Luna could do it every day if she wanted, but this might be Flora's only chance for adventure!

As she stood still, she heard the dogs barking—louder and closer than ever before. She tipped her head to listen. The sound was in front of her. She quieted her heart and headed straight for it.

The sound stopped. She put her snout up to sniff. An explorer had to use all her senses to find her way in unfamiliar territory. But the only scent that filled Flora's nose was a green and corny smell. She kept going. The cornfield ended at a road. This one was bigger than the road near the barn. Flora took one cautious step into the sunshine.

"Hike!" someone shouted. Flora tucked herself back into the cornstalks.

"Pull, Oscar, pull," the voice said. "Show these young pups how to make it fly."

Pulling? This she had to see. Flora poked her head out.

A team of animals, five in all, was coming up the road. They were hooked together on either side of a rope. In a stream of black, white, yellow, and brown fur, the animals flowed forward, pulling steadily against harnesses at their shoulders.

So these must be dogs!

"Come on, Oscar, pull!" the voice said.

Flora gazed at the long snouts and flowing tails. She watched as the many-colored faces drew near.

Pink tongues flapped and rolled over sharp white teeth. Ears were tipped back. But it was the eyes that stopped Flora's heart. Bright. Determined. Proud.

Flora wondered if her eyes would ever look like that.

At the end of the line was a man riding on a cart with four wheels that clattered and bounced over the gravel road. Dark hair covered his face, and he looked fierce.

"Hike!" The man cracked a whip, and the dogs pressed on with new energy.

There was one dog in the lead, and his ears picked up slightly as his eyes rested on Flora. He seemed to be taking in that she was out of place, but he didn't break his stride. The other dogs in the line now glanced at her. Flora's knees trembled. She knew that she should run away, but she was mesmerized. There was something in the teamwork, in the purpose and effort that they shared, that made it hard for her to breathe.

Would her brothers ever consider trying this? Being a *team?*

The man caught sight of her. "Whoa!" he shouted, and pulled back on a lever that made the wheels stop moving. The dogs halted.

"Dabnabbit! Every time we start the strength training, something happens. Why are you out of your pen, little piggy? Somebody needs to learn a lesson."

Although the dogs had pulled in silence, now they stamped and whined and barked. They clearly didn't like being stopped.

Only the lead dog was calm. His eyes were still on Flora, and she could now see they were soft blue with a black pupil in the middle. This must be Oscar.

She watched as his tongue pulsed in and out with each breath. She stuck her tongue out and tried it, but it felt strange. What was it supposed to do for her?

The man stepped off the cart and slowly approached Flora. "This'll be the only time I find you out of your pen. Guaranteed!" He stretched out his hands. "C'mere, piggy."

Uh-oh. This looked like trouble.

Flora thought fast and skittered sideways out of reach, just as the man lunged down to grab her.

"Confound it!" he yelled. "Don't make me set these dogs on you."

She dashed around to the other side of the team and caught sight of their sharp teeth. Loose dogs would be more trouble than she could handle—plan or no plan. Then why was she still standing near them? Something made her want to stay close. These dogs were determined, excited, but not angry or mean. They were eager to get back to their job.

What Flora really wanted to do was ask them some questions. She hustled closer, then stopped. Two dogs barked and yanked sideways against their harnesses. The cart shifted, and the man walked back to steady it. The barkers kept up their noise. Only Oscar stood stock-still, moving just his head to watch Flora. She took a few steps back. No one seemed to be in a talking mood.

The man came around the cart. "Stop running in circles, you little barnyard bonehead." He stepped toward her, hands out.

Flora skipped out of reach again—this time farther up the road.

"Fine." The man stomped back onto the cart. "I'll catch you later."

He grabbed up the dog lines, and the cart started to roll. "Hike!" he shouted. Oscar and the others jumped against their harnesses. They pushed forward, and the cart gained speed.

Wow. Flora's heart raced.

The whole operation barreled in her direction. Flora began to run alongside. She stuck her tongue out sideways and lunged with each step as if she were pushing against her own harness.

"Hike, piggy!" shouted the man. Flora glanced over her shoulder. The man's angry frown was replaced by a grin. "So you're a runner! Come on, you little breakout artist, keep up! It's training time!"

The encouraging words went right to her head. What a feeling it would be to run with a team. She imagined herself at the head of a long pack of dogs. Flora surged again. She concentrated on putting not just speed but power into each stride. Flora threw her head down and skittered as fast as she could.

But the dogs were much faster. She was soon running next to the cart.

"Hike!" the man shouted down to her. Flora didn't want to give up. But she was winded now. Her legs weren't as strong as her determination. She fell behind and had to breathe their dust.

Up ahead, the cart stopped, and the man set the lever against the wheels. The dogs began barking again. Flora threw herself down on a patch of grass at the side of the road, heaving and gasping.

"You've got spirit, don't you?" the man asked, walking over to her.

This time she had no energy to run away. Soon she felt strong fingers rub the top of her head and behind her ears. Flora had never felt anything so delicious. The man bent his face close, and she tried to reach up and lick it.

"Troublemaker," said the man. "Cute, but a big troublemaker."

Flora didn't even struggle when he carried her to the cart.

"Hike!" the man shouted again.

A moment later, Flora was moving faster than she ever had. The wind rushing past her ears felt wonderful. Unfortunately, the team was headed back toward her pen.

Stop! Turn around! she wanted to shout. She tried to wiggle free. *Don't end my adventure this soon!*

Chapter 7

It was no use. Flora was plopped back in her pen, where everyone was huddled together in a corner. Her brothers jumped up and ran over to her, all asking at the same time where she'd been.

Flora sprawled in the dirt.

"Children, calm down." Mother stepped into the crowd and nosed Flora in the leg, sniffing her gently. "Flora's been in the cornfield," she announced. She sniffed again. "And she had a run-in with dogs. Flora, honey, are you all right? Did they hurt you? What made you run out into that wild world?"

Flora took a deep breath and unsteadily got to her hooves. She watched the man with the beard walk back to their pen with a hammer in hand.

"I—I just wanted a look around." Flora wasn't sure if Mother would change from being worried to angry. "I leaned against a board and it broke, so I decided to take a walk."

There was a cracking sound. Everyone looked over to see the man toss the broken board into the junk heap.

"Children, stay away from the opening." Mother shooed her family into the corner. "Remember, there's nothing but danger and trouble out there."

The man dragged a new board over and began nailing it in place.

"Did the dogs attack you in the cornfield?" Alfred asked.

"They're not attacking dogs," said Flora, "and they don't go into the cornfield. They're pulling dogs." She looked around at the staring eyes. This must be how Luna felt when Flora was looking at her. For the first time in her life she was the one who had a story to tell.

"It happened like this . . ."

No one interrupted, and Flora told the truth except for the part where she fell behind. In her story, Flora ran flank to flank with the pulling dogs, her hooves pounding the road as she matched her running companions step for galloping step.

"That sounds even better than digging up a nail," Alfred said. "You are the bravest pig ever."

"A pig needs to be careful, not brave, Alfred," said Mother. "There won't be any more digging up nails, and . . . let's just see how well the farmer fixed the fence." She walked over to the new board and pushed against it with her whole body. Then she turned and faced her children. "It's sufficient. So there won't be any more narrow escapes from packs of running dogs, either. I'm sure Flora understands how close she came to disaster. She won't be so foolish and reckless next time."

Next time, thought Flora. *I can't wait.*

* * *

Flora was excited to tell Luna about her adventure, and her chance came at naptime the following day.

"I got out and went for a run in the wild outside!" she said when Luna jumped up on her post.

"That's what I heard." Luna wrapped her tail around her feet. "And just how wild was it out there?"

"Getting out was amazing!" she said. "Actually, I spent most of my time in the cornfield, which is an excellent place for hiding, but the best part was running with the dogs."

"Hmm." The tip of Luna's tail twitched. "Were they barking and slobbering and sticking their tongues out all over their faces?"

Flora sat down. She remembered now that Luna didn't have nice things to say about dogs. She was right about the tongues and the barking, but Flora also remembered the way their strong legs never gave up and the blue eyes of the lead dog. She wanted to run with them again. "Why don't you like dogs?" she asked.

Luna yawned. "Dogs think cats are useless, which is a lie. They also think cats are lazy, which is true. Cats can't wait to sleep, and dogs can't wait to do stuff. They try too hard. The people who live in the house say that in a couple of months someone will come along and pay a lot of money for the dogs and take them up to the North Pole, where it is snowy and freezing cold, or down to the South Pole, where it is even colder and truly wild. Meanwhile, I will be spending my days choosing warm places to curl up."

Flora had so many questions, she didn't know where to start. "What is money? Where is the South Pole? And why do people want to go where it's cold?" She stared into Luna's eyes without blinking so the cat would know she was listening—and waiting.

Luna started to give herself a bath, but one look at Flora seemed to change her mind. "I can see we won't be talking about anything else until you learn all you can about this North and South Pole business, so I might as well tell you."

Flora did a little dance with her front feet. Then she forced herself to be still and quiet, not permitting even one ear twitch or snout tremble.

"No food can grow in the poles," started Luna. "No corn. No vegetables. No nothing. But it doesn't matter, because humans—well, some humans—like being where life is difficult and wild." Luna let out a disgusted sniff. "These humans love to go to the poles to be truly miserable so they can come home and tell stories, and the dogs love to go so they can pull a sled every day. These polar sleds carry heavy loads that don't feel heavy once they get moving because they slide along on their runners that are slick and fast. Everyone works hard and works as a team. The ones that don't, die. That's what people say, anyway, when they're sitting around the fire at night talking, which is an excellent time for getting good ear rubs . . ."

Flora made herself stay silent as Luna talked and talked, until the pig family woke up and started nosing around and asking Flora to teach them a new game.

"A pulling game," said Alfred.

"See you next time." Luna slipped off her post to the other side of the fence.

Flora stuck her eye up to a crack between the boards so she could see her friend. "When you come back, will you tell me more stories about the poles? And . . . do you think I'll ever have another adventure?"

"You just keep up your spirit. Trouble comes to us all. Adventure comes to those who choose it but turns into trouble quick if you don't know how to land on your feet."

That night, Flora dreamed about the freezing-cold poles. In her dream, she lived in a house of snow. She shared stories with her team. And she pulled a sled.

In the middle of the night, she woke up and walked to the top of the manure pile to see what had awakened her. A great yellow circle above the cornfield had slipped out from behind some clouds. The moon. It was the first moon Flora had ever seen. Her heart filled with the beauty of it, and she made a promise to herself. *I will be prepared. And I won't live forever inside this pen.*

Chapter 8

The days gradually cooled, but the fire in Flora's heart didn't. Since her escape, each day at naptime, Flora walked around leaning and pushing against every single fence board as she listened for squeaks and creaks. But it was no use. There weren't any loose planks. The man with the beard had made sure of that.

It was hard not to get discouraged. Flora's only brush with adventure these days came from listening to Luna's stories. Luna went in and out of the farmhouse whenever she wanted, paying attention when the people talked. She had plenty to report.

One time, Luna told Flora that fire was like magic to people. As soon as there was a fire in the fireplace, they would gather around and stare into it. The fire seemed to fill up their heads with memories and words, so many they'd come tumbling out.

Flora loved Luna's stories, but she also asked plenty of questions about her own interests. Flora wanted to know about oceans and icebergs, ships and storms. She wanted to know about the ocean's creatures, such as what an octopus looked like. Eight legs? Like a giant underwater spider? Impossible . . . and thrilling. Some days Luna was more talkative than others, and on those days, Flora even asked about dogs and sleds.

When Luna wasn't around, Flora practiced landing on her feet with a game she introduced to her brothers called Keep Your Hoof-Side Down. Everyone was supposed to take turns leaping and twisting in the air and still land standing up. But the game never caught on.

Maybe her brothers didn't like the game because they were getting too big. They were all eating solid food now from the trough, which made the shoving at mealtime an even mightier struggle. Mother needed her share too, and she was bigger than them all by far.

Then one day, the farmer opened a gate at the back of the pigpen that had never been open before. Flora bounded through as soon as she saw what was happening.

"We're free!" she squealed. Then she noticed that her freedom was just another pen, only smaller. "Never mind—it's still a cage."

Flora looked back at her family. Snouts crowded and sniffed at the gate, but no one stepped through.

"Anyway," Flora said as she started exploring the corners, "at least it's new. There has to be stuff to dig up in here."

The farmer stepped into the old pen and began to shoo and shove Flora's mother into the new pen. Mother clearly didn't like it. "I have a bad feeling about this, children. Hold your ground, and Flora, get back home."

Mother locked her knees against the farmer's pushing, and Flora joined her brothers in milling around Mother's legs. But when the farmer stepped out and returned with a stick, Mother and all her children surged into the new pen.

"It's okay. At least we're together." Flora started running her nose close to the ground along the fence line. "The best way to know where to dig is to use your snout. At least that's my plan."

"Look who else has a plan," said Mother. Flora glanced up to see the farmer tying Mother to the fence with a rope around her neck.

"Mama!" screeched Flora. "What's happening?" She rushed up to her mother. "Pull away. Break the rope."

Mother pulled, but neither the rope nor the fence gave an inch. "I'm stuck, children," she called. "Stay close to me." Flora and her brothers crowded around her legs. The farmer walked through the open gate to the old pen and poured a bucket of delicious slops into the trough. They not only heard it; they smelled it too.

"Dinner!" squealed her brothers, and they went dashing home to eat.

"Come back!" Flora yelled.

"Children!" Mother pulled against her rope again. "Don't leave my side. It's a trick."

Alfred stopped in the entrance. He looked back

and forth. Then he seemed to make up his mind. "I'm hungry," he whined. "I'll come right back."

Flora could hear the slurping and pushing. "You guys are so dumb!" she hollered. She rubbed against Mother the way Luna would rub against her.

Just then the farmer stepped back inside the new pen and closed the gate. He moved toward Flora.

"Run, Flora!" called Mother.

Flora backed in under Mother's belly instead.

Large hands reached in and grabbed one of Flora's rear legs.

"Get away, Flora!" Mother pushed against the hands with her body, but the farmer easily dragged Flora out, picked her up, and dumped her with her brothers.

They had finished eating and now stood sniffing at the dividing fence.

"Mama!" Alfred cried. "Why did they take you away?" He hit the fence with his little hooves. "I need you!"

"You don't need me, honey. Now, stop making all that fuss."

Alfred dropped down to the ground and put his snout under the gate. Flora nudged his shoulder. "It's okay," she whispered, and tried to make her snout stop quivering.

Mother put her front feet on the fence and looked over at her children.

"You're untied!" Flora tried to reach her mother's face, but she was too short.

"Yes, I am," said Mother. "And you are all big enough to be on your own now."

Alfred whimpered.

"Anyway, I'm right next to you."

"Mama," Flora said, her voice wavering, "why did they do that? Why did they move you?"

Mother dropped back down. "Listen carefully, children. We are farm pigs, and farm pigs are not in control of their lives. Our food is brought to us each day, and if we ask for more than that, it will just make us unhappy and ill-tempered."

Flora led Alfred over to the trough to find a comforting morsel. It was cleaned out except for a bit of pumpkin that had fallen down between the trough and fence. Once he was done eating the snack and had fallen asleep for his nap, Flora climbed the manure pile to think about Mother's words. When Luna came to visit, Flora had extra questions.

"Why aren't farm pigs in control of their lives?" she asked as soon as Luna was settled.

Luna looked at Flora and twitched her tail. "You look as though you've been thinking about this pretty hard. What happened?"

"Mama got moved out of our pen!" Flora stamped her feet. "Why do dogs and cats get to be in control of their lives and pigs don't?"

Luna shook her head. "Dogs make me jump into trees, and horses and cows will step on me if I'm not careful. I never know where my next meal is going to come from."

"But you get to listen to stories. And dogs get to have adventures."

"Dogs live at the end of ropes and leashes and harnesses. Yet nobody is happier than a slobbery dog. The trick is to have *some* control, enough so your life is satisfying and—"

Bang!

A terrific thump shook the ground. Luna flew off her post and out of sight. Flora turned in circles trying to figure out where the sound had come from. Her brothers were awake now and wide-eyed.

Bang!

It sounded like the farmer's hammer, only much louder. It seemed to be coming from the horse stalls on the other side of the shed. Flora had almost forgotten about Nessie because she was such a quiet horse, but not today. Flora tried to see what was happening through the shadows of the shed.

"Mama!" Alfred called.

"Children!" called Mother. "Go to the far corner and stay there. Nessie is having a tantrum."

Flora stayed where she was. This she really wanted to see. She gazed harder into the shadows. Human shouts came from the cornfield, and two men came running.

"Open the stall door before she hurts herself!" one of them called.

Flora watched the broken gate swing open. As Nessie was backed out, her powerful hind legs struck high, breathtaking kicks that looked as though they could bring the barn down if they connected. One of the men tossed a blanket over her head, and suddenly she went quiet. Flora heard him murmuring in a low voice. The other man checked out the gate.

Flora ran down the manure pile. "Mama, what was Nessie trying to do?"

"Oh, honey," Mother said. Her brothers gathered around to listen. "I heard that Nessie doesn't like being in that stall for too long, and when she feels forgotten, her mean streak flares up."

Flora's brothers went back to their naps, but Flora took a seat on the manure pile and wondered at the power of those kicks—and the feelings that inspired them.

Chapter 9

That afternoon, while the men worked to repair Nessie's stall door, Flora thought up a plan to get Mother back. She would ask Nessie to come over and break down the fence. Luna could take her the message.

As Flora gave this plan some more thought, she sorted through the leftovers in the slop trough and found four corncobs with the good stuff all chewed off. "Gather around, everyone!" she called. "I've got a new game called Feelin' Kicky."

She and her brothers were going to get strong. Then if Nessie wasn't willing or able, maybe they could break down the fence themselves.

"Here's what you do," Flora announced. "Toss the cob as high as you can, like this." She took the corncob in her mouth and jerked it into the air. "Then you run to the fence, turn and kick it really hard, run back, and try to stomp the cob before it stops rolling."

She glanced at Alfred. For the first time since Mother had been taken away, he looked a little happy.

"I'll go first." She tossed the corncob and dashed over to the fence. She spun around and reared up on her front legs as her back hooves flashed out behind her. *Tap, tap!* They clicked against the fence. She was hoping for a louder, thumpier sound, but she tore back to the cob that was still rolling and jumped on it with her front hooves.

"There, like that!" Flora spun again and then looked around at her brothers while she caught her breath.

"Wow," Alfred said.

They all lined up behind the corncobs to take a turn. Her brothers cheered one another, especially when the moment came to bang their little hooves into the fence. They played Feelin' Kicky the rest of the afternoon.

The next morning, Flora got up before everyone else. She walked to the fence, stood for a moment, then spun quickly, and kicked. It might have been her imagination, but it felt as if the boards trembled a little.

She wished she could show Luna. She ran up the manure pile to see if her friend was anywhere around. Instead, she saw a big truck backing down the gravel road. It came to a stop in a cloud of dust just on the other side of the junk heap, and the wind brought the smell of its exhaust.

One by one, her brothers woke and wandered over, peeking with their sleepy eyes between boards.

It wasn't until the engine suddenly quieted that Flora heard the dogs. It sounded like hundreds of them, barking and whining from inside the back of the truck, which was covered by a stained, greasy canvas. Two strangers and the man with the dark beard came around the corner of the truck and strode purposefully toward the pigpen.

What was this? Flora could hardly breathe.

"Don't let them catch you!" Mother called from her pen. "Stick together and dash from corner to corner."

Flora looked at Alfred. Alfred hurried over and glued himself to Flora's side. She nuzzled him for encouragement. "Get ready," she whispered.

Two of the men stepped over the fence and into the pen. They lunged and grabbed as Flora and her brothers ran to the farthest corner and jammed themselves into a tight bunch. As soon as the men came close, they ran again, grunting and squealing, to the next corner.

"That's it!" cried Mother. She was standing and looking over the top of the gate. She sounded frantic. "Stay together, children!"

Was that why they moved her out of the pen, Flora wondered, so she couldn't protect her children? The gate between the two pens shuddered. It was Mother throwing herself against the boards.

"Don't let them put their hands on you!" she shouted. "Don't let them pick you up!"

The third man lunged at Flora. She jumped sideways to dodge his hands. Even though she was the smallest pig now, she was faster than her brothers. Her strong back legs powered her forward through the gap between his legs.

She glanced around. The man with the beard fell on Alfred.

"No!" Flora shouted. She dashed over, aimed for the man's head, spun, and kicked backwards.

"Ow. Hey, it's you again," he said.

She could tell she missed his head, but the man let Alfred go.

The three men dusted themselves off. Flora's mother was still shouting encouragement, but Flora's attention suddenly slipped.

The dogs in the truck had kept up their barking. Were they the same dogs from her day in the cornfield? They sounded similarly excited but happy, too, as though they were finally off on the adventure they had been training for.

Adventure.

Did she dare?

This time when the men slowly advanced with their hands out in front, Flora only pretended to scramble. She darted one way and then turned back. Her brothers, including Alfred, all made a break for the other side of the pen. But Flora stood her ground.

"Flora, run!" cried her mother.

"Get that one!" the man with the beard shouted. "She's nothing but trouble."

The men closed in from three sides, and Flora stamped her front feet. She kicked one of her back legs. But she did not run. And when they fell on her and picked her up, she did not struggle.

"Flora!" Alfred squealed.

"Goodbye!" she shouted. "Don't worry about me. Alfred, work hard at your kicking."

The men hoisted Flora out of the pen. The truck growled. Dark smoke leaped from a rattling pipe. Flora shivered.

"You've got yourself a good one there," she heard the man with the beard say. The rest of his words were drowned out as a flap in the dark canvas was flipped up and Flora was shoved into a wood and wire crate.

Chapter 10

Flora felt a quick arrow of sadness stab her. This was no run in the cornfield.

Mother! Alfred! Would she ever see her family again? If she had a howl in her, this would be the time to let it out.

All she could do was squeal.

The air inside the truck was warm. It was filled with the smell of dog and gasoline, and the sound of barking was now deafening. The truck growled deeply and moved with a lurch. Flora was thrown against the metal grid of her cage. Judging from the yelps around her, so were her traveling companions.

The barking stopped. Flora picked herself up as the truck crunched along the gravel road. It vibrated and shook and went over heavy bumps now and then, which made it hard for Flora to keep her footing. She kept knocking her head. Then, after a bone-cracking heave that lifted every cage into the air and slammed them back down, the ride smoothed out.

Flora was definitely scared, but she had picked her moment, and she had shown spirit and courage. Luna would be so proud.

Luna! Flora didn't even get to say goodbye.

Flora looked around her cage. A dirty, crumpled blanket lay on the floor, and two metal pans were upturned. There might have been water in one of them until the big heave. Now there was just a wet spot on a corner of the blanket. Beside the other bowl were two carrots and half an apple.

If only Alfred were here with her.

No. It was a good thing her little brother was safe in the pen.

Of course Luna would be just fine. She was

happiest telling stories, except now she would have to find someone else to listen to them.

Daylight flashed in through the corners of the canvas sides. In the flashes, she caught glimpses of the dogs. She watched as some of them circled inside their cages before lying down. There were perhaps ten or fifteen altogether, and they didn't seem afraid or worried.

"Oscar?" she said. It was the only name she knew. "Is Oscar here?" she said louder, though she doubted anyone could hear her over the truck's roar. There was no answer.

Whether these dogs were from the farm or not, Flora was sure she was the only pig. Judging by how hard the men had worked to catch her or one of her brothers, there must be a need for a strong and fast pig on this adventure. No pig on the farm was stronger or faster than she was.

The drone of the wheels made Flora sleepy. She circled on her blanket as she had seen the dogs do and then flopped down.

* * *

Boom!

Flora's eyes opened.

Crash!

Thunk.

She scrambled to her feet. The truck had stopped moving.

Men were shouting to one another.

The flap at the back of the truck suddenly opened, and light poured in. Two men reached into Flora's cage, lifted her out, and placed her on solid ground. She rocked a bit, getting used to the feel of a steady surface again. Hands fumbled around her neck, buckling up a leather collar and then chaining it to a short post. The dogs were lifted from the truck one by one, still inside their cages. Then the truck roared away louder than ever.

At first, Flora had trouble opening her eyes. The world was too bright. But by squinting, she slowly got used to it.

The dock was busier than a pigpen full of

piglets and noisier than a truck full of dogs. Men in heavy boots stomped here and there. They carried, rolled, and pushed boxes and barrels from one pile to another. A ship with a thundering engine pulled alongside the dock. Waves sloshed as the men tied the ship down as if it were a living thing that might escape. On top of the post sat a white bird, staring at her.

"Hello," said Flora.

The bird squawked and flew off.

Flora turned her head. In one direction were the piles of boxes and crates and cages. She couldn't see inside any of them. In another direction, there was nothing but blue sparkling water.

This had to be the ocean Luna described! Who would have thought Flora would someday be here, listening to the waves and actually seeing them? And the *smells!*

Luna hadn't told her about the fish smell or the smell of the oily dark wood that she was standing on, plus there was the smell of garbage and, of course, the salty sea. A manure pile smelled fresh and clean compared to this. But Flora liked it. To her, it was the smell of adventure.

"Slide out the gangplank!" a sailor bellowed. A great board banged down from the ship onto the dock, and soon men were filing up it carrying barrels and boxes.

Crash!

Flora jumped. A large wooden box had been slammed to the ground behind her, almost crushing her tail. But the men didn't seem to notice or care.

Only the ringing of a big bell finally made them stop and look around. They seemed to relax and breathe easier, and they addressed one another for the first time that day. Lunch boxes appeared in strong hands, and the men sat in small groups. They tore at their sandwiches as Flora watched.

That was better. Now Flora could think, maybe even talk to someone.

She took a dainty step. Her chain was just long enough that she could see into the first cage. The eyes that looked back were soft blue with black in the middle. Flora blinked. It was Oscar from the farm. She didn't remember him being so large, nor that he had strictly black and white fur. He blinked back when he saw her.

Flora cleared her throat. "Good morning. It's nice to see you again. You're Oscar, right? My name is Flora."

The dog blinked again. "That's right, I'm Oscar. Good morning."

Oscar had a deep, smooth voice. Flora hoped he

would feel like talking. "Do you know what happens next?"

Oscar looked Flora over. It wasn't an unfriendly looking over, but slow and thoughtful, as if he weren't sure he should be talking to a pig.

"Yup," he said finally, "we get on a ship and sail away."

"That ship?" asked Flora.

"That's it." Oscar flipped his nose toward the ship tied to the dock. "The *Explorer*."

"The *Explorer*?" A thrill went from Flora's shoulders down to her hooves. "That sounds very exciting. And what is it we'll be exploring?"

Oscar sat up. "We are going to be the first expedition ever to cross the Antarctic. I've already been there. To get ready for the journey, I went with a team months ago to make food drops."

Flora was confused. "But didn't I see you on the farm the day I escaped my pen?"

Oscar raised his eyebrows. "Oh, so that's why

you look familiar. Yes, that was me. When I'm not leading a team, I train young dogs."

"Only this time, you'll be pulling a sled, right?"

"Yup. That one over there."

Flora looked. Resting on a cement platform was a wooden sled with curved runners, sweeping diagonal frame pieces, and a long, narrow bed for carrying a load. Flora imagined dogs pulling it over the snow. It looked nothing like the cart with wheels back on the farm.

"Wow," she breathed. "Is it fast?"

"Depends on the strength of the team."

No wonder the men had grabbed her. They really did need a strong, fast pig. Flora waited for Oscar to say more, but he was silent. She tried to think of a question to get him talking again.

"Do you like being a sled dog?" she asked.

"Well, that's like asking if a bird likes to fly. Being a sled dog is what I was born to do," said Oscar. "You have to be willing to work hard and get cold and tired. You have to be just a little bit crazy, but at the end of the day, you know you got the pulling done and earned your supper. There's no better job on earth."

Flora was enchanted. She tried to imagine herself running ahead of the team while they were acting just a little bit crazy. "When we get to the Antarctic, do you think you could show me a few things about being a sled dog?" she blurted out.

Before Flora could hear the answer, the other dogs burst out with a great barking and snarling and even began digging and biting at their wire doors.

Flora looked around, heart pounding. What could be the matter?

Chapter 11

The reason for the excitement was a small orange cat.

Walking with its back arched, the cat stared into each cage as if seeking the insults and threats flying her way—as though they gave her power. She stopped in front of Oscar's cage. Oscar did not bark.

The cat licked her chest twice. "Cat attack," she said, and gazed at Oscar, daring him to lunge. He didn't move.

Flora was impressed. Clearly Oscar was a born leader with too much self-control to carry on like a common barnyard dog. And here was someone else to talk with. She cleared her throat.

The cat looked over.

"Hello," said Flora. "Pleased to meet you. My name is Flora, and this is my new friend, Oscar."

The cat walked around Flora, slowly viewing her from every angle. "Nice chain you got there. What kind of joke is a pig, anyway? You're like the mammal version of a frog. No hair, no claws, no horns. No attack weapons and no defense. What is the point?"

How rude! And Flora wanted to tell this cat so. But she wanted her questions answered even more. So she said, "Maybe frogs have qualities that make up for not having those other things. Pigs are known for their spirit."

"Spirit. Oooh yeah. That makes up for everything." The orange cat walked in front of Flora's face, and her fluffy tail brushed Flora's nose. "If you ever get attacked, you can lash out with your spirit."

Flora wasn't sure what to do in the face of such unpleasantness. Still, she had so many questions. "Are you part of the team?"

"Team?" The cat's back arched again. "A cat is never part of a team. A cat is a team unto herself. A cat hardly knows the meaning of the word *team*. A cat looks down on—"

Oscar growled.

It was very low and soft, but it stopped the cat from continuing.

"Never mind, then. I am Sophia. Sophia is the sheriff of this dock. Sophia is the terror of mice, the killer of rats, and she works alone. By the way, have you seen any?"

"Any what?" Flora asked.

"Rats."

"No."

"That's right. This dock is a rat-free zone, thanks to weaponry that others can only dream of." Sophia flexed one set of claws. "Have you heard of the killer instinct? Of course you have, and Sophia's reputation alone is enough to keep the vermin away."

Flora hadn't heard of the killer instinct, but

she didn't let on. "If your work here is finished, per-haps they have work for you on the *Explorer*. You could be very useful. Oscar is a sled dog, and I . . . well, I am ready to help in any way I can on our adventure."

"Heavens, no," said Sophia. "I wouldn't be caught dead on a ship. Cats don't like going on ad-ventures, taking orders, or crossing over water." She shuddered.

Flora thought back to what put Luna in a good mood. "Your fur looks very soft and clean."

Sophia sat down, lifted a front paw, and licked it.

Flora tried again. "Maybe you could tell us what you've heard about the *Explorer* and the crew."

"Sorry. Sophia wishes she could stay and chat, but she's gotta—"

Just then a shadow fell on the company of three, and they looked up. A skinny boy had walked over to them. He glanced around, then sneaked a bit of bread and cheese out of his pocket and stuffed it into his mouth.

Sophia rubbed up against his legs. He bent down and stroked her back. Sophia winked at Flora and arched herself into his hands.

The boy looked in at Oscar. "Hello, big guy." He gently stroked the paw that was sticking out from under the door of the cage. Oscar put his head close to the wire and received a good scratch behind his ears, causing him to half-close his eyes. "Are you ready for an adventure?" the boy asked.

Oh, how Flora loved that word *adventure,* and how she wished those hands were scratching her ears.

As if he could read her thoughts, the boy stood up and took a step over to where she sat. "And a pig," he said, squatting next to her and running his hand down her back. Flora wasn't sure if she should lean on him the way Sophia did or just sit still. As his fingers scratched a spot behind her front left leg, Flora collapsed on the ground and grunted in pleasure.

"A pig, a cat, and dogs. This ship is a zoo," said

the boy. Sophia rubbed against him, not used to being ignored and then jumped into the boy's arms, making him stand up and laugh. "I bet you'd like to be my cat."

Flora grunted again. This cat wasn't even *going* on the ship. She wished she could tell him that.

Just then the bell started ringing. Men hurried by, stuffing last bites of sandwich into their mouths and wiping their hands on their pants.

"Hey, Aleric!" someone yelled.

The boy set Sophia down.

"Get your skinny behind over here and take these boxes to the hold. Nobody sails on this boat for free, you know."

Flora felt her chest filling with pride. Just as she thought, they had an important job in mind for her. *Nobody* sailed for free.

The boy scurried over to a pile of boxes and lifted one. It looked heavy.

"What's a hold?" asked Flora.

"Bottom of the boat," said Oscar. "That's where

they put anything they don't want to think about until they need it."

Aleric staggered onto the ship, through a dark doorway, and out of sight. The three animals watched him go. Flora was afraid Sophia might decide to leave too. "I think he liked you," she said.

Sophia licked herself. "No one can resist a cat."

"What's your secret?"

"Too many questions, sister." Sophia's tail twitched, and she began to walk away.

"Wait!" Flora called. "Just one more."

Sophia paused. Flora rushed on before the cat could change her mind. "You've watched ships leave these docks before, right?"

"Hundreds," said the cat.

"Then you can probably tell me, why am I going on this ship? Do I have a job? What's my job?"

"Oh, you have a job," said the cat. "No extras here. On an expedition, everybody has a purpose."

She turned to go. "But some purposes are better than others."

"Hey, what's that sup-posed to mean?"

"Sheriff needs to be off on her rounds. Goodbye for now."

Flora called after her. "Or forever!" Sophia disappeared between two barrels.

"Well," said Flora to Oscar, "she's kind of inter-esting, and a little mysterious."

Oscar raised his eyebrows and blinked. "Pretty much stuck up and all about herself, if you ask me. But she's a cat, so whattaya gonna do?"

"Oscar, I want you to know, if I can help you in any way, I would be a hard worker, a good team member, and I never complain. And in case they separate us and I don't get to talk to you, I want to say right now, good luck."

Once again Oscar looked Flora over. She couldn't be sure, but he seemed a little bit sad. Then he rested his head on his paws. "You be careful."

"Sure, you too." Flora nodded. Thanks to Luna, she was ready to land on her feet. If only someone would tell her about her job, it would make it a lot easier to prepare.

After the hours of truck noise and a day of dock bustle, night floated down as soft and quiet as a bird's feather. All that could be heard was the gentle splashing of waves. Flora felt as though she might be the only one awake. She looked up into the clear night sky and . . . there they were.

Stars. She'd had no idea there would be so many, and they doubled themselves by reflecting off the water. Some were bigger and brighter than others, and they almost blinked if one watched them long enough.

Eyes watching over me, thought Flora.

Her mind went back to her mother and brothers

on the farm. For just a moment, she missed the cozy pigpen and her family. She imagined her brothers sleeping on one another for company. She hoped Mother and Alfred were together again. Maybe Luna was looking up at the same stars. Flora wondered if her friend missed her at all.

As she fell asleep, Flora thought of what Luna had told her about snow. She dreamed that Antarctic snow was falling. The team was struggling to move the sled forward. Paws were slipping. All around her, dogs were stumbling. Only one sled puller had any traction—the one with hooves. Hike!

Chapter 12

"Load up the dogs! Move it! You there, be of use or get out of the way!"

Flora woke to someone shouting, and to bright sunlight. A moment later, she was being led toward the ship, the salty air tickling her nose.

"Bye, Oscar!" she called over her shoulder. "See you on board."

She was so happy to be truly starting her adventure, she could put up with anything—even the sailor's rough tug on the chain around her neck as they went up and into the ship, past rows of empty cages on either side, each with a soft-looking blanket.

Which one was hers? Maybe her blanket would have a picture of a pig or a star on it.

She kept stopping to look and sniff, but the sailor kept yanking her forward. She hoped he wouldn't shove her into a cage on the end. She enjoyed company, and if she had two friendly neighbors, she might be able to get sled-pulling tips from them.

They walked past the last cage on deck. Flora tried to turn around. There must be some mistake. But as she protested, the sailor dragged her through a dark doorway. A steep staircase stretched in front of her into the gloom below.

This must be the hold. Why was he taking her there? What about her soft blanket? Her cage among the members of the dog team? Flora locked her legs and pulled back with all her strength, but she was forced to hop down each step, behind her clanking chain. The shouting and banging from the world above got more and more muffled as she went down.

At the bottom of the stairs, the sailor walked a few paces in and clipped her chain to a box. She didn't turn to watch as he clomped back up. She just listened. Then she was alone.

Flora blinked.

The only light in the hold came from the opening at the top of the stairs. Her chain clinked and her thoughts whirled as she looked for a blanket. There wasn't one. She slumped onto the hardwood floor and put her chin between her front hooves.

Something rustled.

She lifted her head and called softly, "Hello?"

Nobody answered. The hold was where they put things they didn't want to think about . . . until they needed them. That was what Oscar had said. Wait a minute—she wasn't a box of tools or a barrel of cheese. How long would it take them to realize she'd been chained below by mistake? Oscar and the other sled dogs were up in the fresh air, so why wasn't she?

She laid her head back down and tried to imagine what advice Luna would give her. Flora could hear her friend say, "Adventure quickly turns into trouble."

Sighing, Flora tried to think more positively, until a clatter distracted her. A sailor with a box in his arms pounded down the wooden stairs, and behind him was another sailor and another. A long line of men darkened the doorway, each with a box or barrel or sack.

She hopped up. She wanted to make it easy for someone to spot her.

Each time their burdens slammed onto the floor, Flora jumped. The supplies were rolled or shoved or tossed into place, and then the men banged up the stairs, only to return with another load.

They were all business and spoke only when they needed to.

"Cap'n says leave a path."

"Cap'n says stack 'em only two high."

"Strap down those barrels. There're rough seas between here and there. Cap'n says the precious cargo down here will be the difference between life and death once the expedition starts."

Precious cargo? Maybe the captain would come down next and inspect his supplies and his pig. He sounded like a person who could sort this out.

The parade of men finally ended without a single one of them noticing or speaking to her or scratching her head. The last man disappeared through the doorway, and Flora was alone again.

Was it possible . . . could she be the precious cargo? Being put down here had to have something to do with being special. Or maybe it had to do with the training a sled pig needed. Yes, that was it!

She would show the captain her best spirit when he came down to look things over—not just boxes and barrels, but his special pig, too.

Chapter 13

When the ship's horn blew, it felt as though the deep sound went inside Flora and rattled around. Two more blasts came after the first. As soon as the last blast died away, Flora became aware of a low rumble.

The ship's engines were running. A slow side-to-side rocking motion started up and sent a thrill through Flora from the tip of her snout down to the end of her tail, despite her awful quarters.

They were under way!

She looked around at all of the supplies piled against the walls of the ship. Surrounding her was a wide space, a clear walking path to the stairs, and another path through the boxes and barrels. Close by was a food bowl. Flora sniffed it—spaghetti with tomato sauce and rinds of squash. Not bad, but she'd rather explore her new environment.

Unfortunately, Flora couldn't get farther than a few steps before she was stopped short. She walked a few more paces in the other direction until her chain pulled tight. But this time she strained against it, and the chain gave. Behind her she heard the box she was clipped to grind against the floor.

She sat down. This could get tiring.

But wait! That was the point! It was supposed to be hard work. Flora had some catching up to do. Stuck in her pen back home, she hadn't trained nearly as much as the farm dogs.

Flora pulled at her chain again and heard a satisfying growl from the box scraping over the rough wooden decking. Her leather collar dug into her neck. Good. Sled pulling wasn't supposed to be comfortable. Too bad no one was down here to cheer her on and make sure her technique was right.

Instead a smell wrinkled her nose. It was not a good smell. She tried to shut it out. She focused on the window in the door at the top of the stairs, on that small bit of light, and strained again. *Don't . . . give . . . up.*

Step. Pull. Step, step! Stop.

As soon as Flora sat down, she heard that strange rustling again.

"Anybody there?" she asked.

Another rustle, or maybe it was more like scratching, came from behind a box. So did more of that bad smell. Flora shivered.

But this was no time to be afraid like little Alfred. She dragged her box until she could peer into a dark space between cargos. The floor almost seemed to be moving, as if it were alive. Flora looked longingly at the stairs, and when she turned back—

Yikes! She hopped backwards.

A big, greasy rat with long, wiry whiskers and a bald patch between his ears had stepped out from behind a box and was sniffing in Flora's direction.

Flora tried to be brave. She tried to remember her rat-hunting moves, but suddenly attacking a crumpled paper bag or a dried orange peel didn't seem like enough training.

As she watched him creep closer, she worked hard to stop shaking so her chain wouldn't rattle. Then he stood on his hind legs and opened his mouth, showing off his impressive, sharp yellow teeth. He snapped his mouth shut. Then he oozed in the direction of her food bowl.

Flora scrambled as far away as possible and sank to her stomach. She could see him slip over the bowl's edge and paddle around while searching out the best morsels. Evidently he did not care that his fur was becoming soggy with tomato sauce or that this was not his food.

In a moment he was joined by two mean-looking buddies. Chewing and slurping were the only sounds. Flora imagined an ocean of rats watching from the shadows. She hid her face between her hooves.

Once the food in Flora's bowl had been eaten, the rats disappeared. That was good. The light at the top of the stairs was dimming. Night was coming. The rustling in the darkness seemed even louder.

Flora shivered at the thought of having to listen to rat sounds all night long. The ship was bucking and pounding along. She could feel the boards underneath her shudder. She needed to think about something cheerful.

"Hike," she whispered to herself, and brought the pictures to mind. The snow was a glittering blanket. Across the folds of white raced Flora the sled pig. She was galloping beside a frozen lake with a team of a dozen sled dogs. Oscar was in front. At the end of the line was the sled, brightly painted in a festive blue with white stars for decoration.

"Onward!" called Oscar.

"Onward!" Flora echoed. "We're tough! We're brave! And we're a little bit crazy!" She leaped and twisted in the air in a crazy little dance before speeding on.

Even if sleep didn't come, Flora's mind was in a far better place.

"Hike," she murmured again and again.

Chapter 14

The next morning, the door at the top of the stairs opened.

Flora leaped to her feet. *Captain?*

A sailor came down, wearing a dirty apron and holding a bucket of slops. He was a giant of a man with hair on his arms as long and curly as a sheep's and a lower lip that hung open, showing huge uneven teeth.

"The ship's cook wants to check on his bacon maker!" He had a voice like the scraping sound of a shovel on a cement floor. Slobber collected in the corners of his mouth as he talked. "Time for eating, my little pork chop."

When he dumped the slops into her bowl, Flora gladly grabbed a bite. Wonderful! Biscuits with gravy.

"Good piggy. You ate everything from yesterday," he said, patting her on the flank. "Amos likes a big eater."

Flora looked up. If only he knew who the big eaters were around here.

"Amos wants you to grow fat! So fat! So big!" His long arms, which usually hung almost to his knees, were spread wide.

Flora plunged her mouth into the slops. She was on her way to getting stronger. Now she needed to get bigger, too. She looked over the top of the bowl, glancing around for what she knew was waiting and watching.

Sure enough. As soon as the cook's footsteps faded at the top of the stairs, the three rats slipped out from between the boxes. Whiskers. Matted brown fur. Impossibly small, shiny eyes. Their leader, the one with the bald patch, clacked his curved yellow teeth together. *Snap! Snap!*

Taking up the call, the other two clacked their teeth as well, and the ocean of rats she'd imagined the day before started coming out of the shadows.

Flora swallowed a last mouthful, backed up, and locked her trembling knees.

Then the bald rat king hissed.

It was a terrible sound, worse than the teeth clacking. As soon as he did this, the army of rats swarmed over her food, snarling at one another as they cleaned out her bowl. When it was spotless, they slipped away into the shadows—all except for the king. He crawled back into the bowl, sprawled on his back, and began to lick the gravy from his round middle. With every lick she could see his yellow teeth. She could smell him too. It was a sour smell, and Flora guessed that all the licking in the world wouldn't get that stink out.

When he was done, the rat rose up on his hind legs. He opened his mouth and hissed again.

Flora tried to step back farther, but the collar jammed up under her chin. What did he want now?

Thankfully, nothing. He waddled away . . .

Until Amos came downstairs with dinner.

Flora got ready to gulp mouthfuls as soon as the slops hit her bowl. While she swallowed quickly, she kept one eye on the shadows and the other on Amos.

Please stay, she thought.

But as she took her third bite, he clomped off. This time he was only halfway up the stairs when eyes, ears, and whiskers slipped into the dim light.

Flora hurried away, still chewing.

This was too big a challenge. One pig against an army of rats didn't seem at all fair.

That night in her dreams, naked tails snaked across her body and twisted around her neck, choking her.

Chapter 15

Flora woke up the next morning with a terrible headache—but also a change of heart. She staggered to her feet. "Enough!" she said out loud.

Sophia had been wrong when she had said pigs were like frogs. Pigs *did* have weapons. But what were they? Flora paced weakly back and forth. The chain around her neck clanked against the boards at every step. No answer came into her head.

Flora ran her tongue over her teeth. They were great for chewing leftover scrambled eggs and watermelon rinds. But they didn't feel like weapons. And her hooves weren't sharp enough to put a hole through a paper bag unless it was wet.

The door opened.

"Good morning, delicious!" Amos dropped the

food into her bowl and ran his hands over Flora's ribs. "How is Amos's little sausage?" Spit flew from his mouth with every word. And then he was gone.

Flora fixed her gaze on the dark corners as she warily moved over her bowl.

She didn't take a bite.

Slither. Click.

She could hear tails sliding and toenails tapping just out of sight.

Then a low tide of hissing rats flowed forward in a half circle in front of her. Flora realized she was more than five times as big as the largest one. None of them even came up to her chin. That gave her some confidence, but not much.

She wanted to stamp her feet, but she was afraid her trembling knees would collapse. She tried to calm her beating heart.

In the center of the mass, the rat king stepped forward. He opened his mouth impossibly wide, like an enormous yawn, and then brought his teeth together in a loud snap. In the next instant, Flora was attacked.

She swung her head, sending a couple of rats tumbling. But it didn't stop the crush of fur and teeth. Some jumped on her back while others went at her underbelly with sharp bites. She came down hard on her front feet, trying to stomp a hairless tail or two, but the rats were too fast.

Flora scrambled backwards, and as soon as she moved away from the bowl, the rats called off their attack and scurried to get their share of slops. Flora looked down at her shoulders. They were covered with scratches and drops of blood.

She felt dazed. Nothing had prepared her for an enemy so fearsome. Flora recalled Luna's attack on the barn rat. What would Luna do with a whole thieving bunch of ship rats? Well, she wouldn't give up, that's for sure. *I won't give up either,* Flora thought, trying to find the courage to believe the words. *I can't give up—they're eating my only food.*

* * *

Over the next few days, Flora had to be satisfied with a small victory that kept her from starving.

When Big Amos came down with her food, she found she could eat four bites by swallowing without chewing before he clomped away.

By stamping her feet, she could usually keep the rats at bay and grab one more bite before the entire crew gathered. They were brave only in a large group.

She also knew that when she backed off quickly, they would leave her alone.

But all of this meant she still got little to eat. Yet Flora was determined not to give up on her dream. She continued to pull her box back and forth to improve her strength. And sometimes she practiced going a little crazy, prancing on her hind legs, shaking her head, and snorting.

All the while she would whisper to herself, "Don't give up!"

The training always tuckered her out, which

was just as well. It was easier for her to drift off to sleep at the end of the day.

One night, curled up tight to stay warm, she saw two stars appear in the blackness. In her hazy half sleep, she didn't question how stars could come down from the sky and shine in the hold of a ship. She just watched the tiny glimmers of light and re-membered that night on the dock. The two stars twinkled—and then they blinked.

Flora sat up and grunted, her chain clinking softly. Stars didn't blink.

She waited.

The pair of lights developed a furry face around them. "Cat attack," said the face.

"Sophia!" squealed Flora. "You changed your mind. You came with us!"

Chapter 16

Shanghaied!" Sophia yowled. "Kidnapped. Stolen. Forced to come aboard against my free will."

"Join the club." But Flora was so excited, she couldn't keep her front feet still.

"Cats don't join . . ." Sophia glanced over her shoulder. "Never mind."

Something was different about her, Flora thought. Sophia had lost weight. She looked less confident. "Are you all right?" she asked. "You look thin."

"So do you—and definitely hairier."

Flora looked down. Her hair had always been softer than the other pigs' hair on the farm, but now it was growing thicker, covering her body in a coat of white that could almost be called fur.

Sophia picked up a paw and winced. There was a cut on it. "The worst thing about being on this tub is they expect you to work for your supper. I was tucked into a nice warm corner in the kitchen until the cook saw something hiding in the rice bin he didn't like."

Flora had a pretty good idea what it was. The cook was lucky to have Sophia. She'd keep his kitchen rat-free.

The cat went on. "Threw Sophia down here like a moldy, sea-soaked bag of corn. Said I had to make myself useful. Apparently there's a rat problem on this ship that can only be solved by making a cat miserable!"

"It's true." Flora peered into a dark corner. "This ship needs a rat hunter like you."

A scrabble of claws came from the dark. Sophia crouched and stared in the direction of the sound. "Well," she said, "off Sophia goes, then, to do her job."

"Wait! Stay and talk for a little while first." Flora strained against her chain. "You wouldn't believe how lonely it's been."

"Not lonely enough for some of us," Sophia muttered. "Gotta go . . ."

"You're going to do great, you know. You have the perfect skills and weapons."

Sophia shuddered. "Yeah, perfect."

"But I thought you said—"

"I like mice." Sophia flinched and hissed as a rat popped into view for a moment. "Mice practically roll over when you pounce on them."

"But you told me—"

"I might have exaggerated. Actually, Sophia grew up in a house with a carpet and a sun-warmed cushion next to the window. Sophia hates rats."

A loud grinding sound, like teeth on wood, started up close by. Sophia made a noise that seemed to come from deep in her throat. It sounded angry and afraid at the same time.

"You'll get the hang of it," Flora said. She wished she could help somehow.

"Oh, I'm sure I will." Sophia sighed. "I'm a cat, aren't I? I'm not some creature with pebbles instead of paws and teeth as dull as spoons."

Flora ignored the insult. "Well, whenever you need a break from hunting, I'll keep you company."

The cat sniffed. "Too bad I have to go back to work at all, unlike someone else"—she looked straight at Flora—"who gets her food for free."

"I've been working," Flora said. If the cat stuck around, she'd show her just how strong her pulling muscles were getting. "And I would be happy to work more. I'm willing to do practically anything."

Sophia sat back. She no longer seemed eager to go on the prowl.

The tickle of a plan crept into Flora's brain. She sat on her haunches too.

"Look. I can do even better than keep you company. I hate rats as much as you, maybe even more. I bet together . . ." Flora's voice trailed off. She was afraid of sounding ridiculous.

The cat's tail swished. "What are you saying?"

Flora sat up tall. "Pigs are not known for their rat-hunting skills. But no one's ever tried to teach us. I can learn anything, and I would very much like to prove that a pig can be good at important work. Sophia, since you are the rat-hunting sheriff on this ship, I would be proud to be your deputy."

"Cats don't work with others," Sophia said. Then she looked up at Flora. "On the other hand, it's not as though the rat problem on this ship is going to solve itself."

"I want to be useful," said Flora.

"Aren't you forgetting something? You're locked up."

"Not a problem." Flora stretched out her neck.

"Your teeth look just right for cutting through leather."

It took a while and more grumbling, but before too long Flora's chain clanked to the dark floor, the collar chewed in two.

Chapter 17

Taking rat-catching lessons from someone with a different set of equipment was a challenge for Flora. "I don't get it," she said. Deputy and sheriff were in a space behind a stack of boxes that had become their training ground. "Can you explain it again?"

"Crouch, pounce, dig in your claws, and then at the end, bite the neck to finish it off. It's called the death bite, and anyone with a killer instinct knows how to do it." All business, Sophia demonstrated each step with great energy, and when she got to the death-bite part, she attacked a coil of rope. "Like that. Couldn't be simpler."

"Um." Flora didn't want Sophia to think she didn't have the killer instinct. "What will you do while I'm crouching and pouncing and doing . . . the death bites?"

"Sophia will be watching your technique and encouraging you."

"I think the part about digging in the claws is getting me mixed up." Flora stared at her hooves.

"Trust Sophia," said the cat, locking eyes with Flora. "Now, get out there and make me proud."

Flora crept around the corner and crouched. Two rats were chewing on the corner of a box. She gathered herself for the pounce. The wide-bodied one turned and saw her. He bared his teeth.

"Now," whispered Sophia from behind Flora.

Flora tensed her muscles—and leaped!

What happened next was the most embarrassing moment of her life. Her hooves, which might have leaped just fine on dirt or a manure pile, slipped out from under her on the wooden boards. She fell flat on her belly, which knocked the air out of her. As she lay gasping, she thought she might have heard laughter as the rats padded away.

Sophia switched her tail. "At least the crouch was good."

Flora got to her feet. Twice more she crept out to meet her enemy and twice more suffered the same result. The only difference was that each time she pounced with less enthusiasm so as to save her poor belly. She dragged herself back to the sheriff.

"Not bad," said Sophia. "You're starting to get it now."

Flora moaned—and a stream of light flashed down into the dark hold. The rats scurried for the shadows, and Sophia froze. "Who is that?" she asked.

"Just Amos, the cook. Breakfast time. Come

on!" Flora dashed back to her bowl. She threw herself on her chains to disguise that she was no longer bound by them. Sophia curled in behind her.

"How's my little ham bone doing, eh?" Amos dumped out a particularly large helping of leftovers. "I got a big feast for you today. You're still skinny. Get big and fat, okay?" The cook turned and looked around. He tried to see into the dark corners. "Where is that lazy cat?"

Flora felt Sophia curl in closer.

"Amos still has rats in his kitchen!" he boomed, then peered around a few more boxes before heading up the stairs.

"Anything in that bowl for a lazy cat?" whispered Sophia. "Pig food smells pretty good right now."

"Well, don't just sniff it—or smells will be all you'll get," said Flora, plunging her snout into the slops. She managed to bolt down the first bite and get a second one into her mouth while Sophia was still only daintily sniffing.

Snap. Click.

Sophia crouched. She peered. Flora grabbed another bite.

Suddenly, a wave of brown and gray flowed over the deck boards. Sophia jumped three feet in the air. "Run for your life!" she screeched.

Flora backed up, chewing and waiting for the tug of chain. When it didn't come, she remembered she was free.

"Sophia, wait for me!" she called, and trotted away from the hideous sloshing and slurping.

Sophia's hair stood straight out all over her body. "Is that what happens every time?"

"Every day," Flora answered. "I've gotten used to it."

"I had no idea there were so many rats in the whole world."

Flora slumped to the floor. It didn't seem very likely either of them would be getting a full meal anytime soon.

Sophia poked a claw into Flora's back. "Training time is over, Deputy. This is for real."

"Ouch," said Flora. "What's the plan?"

Sophia leaned close to Flora's ear. "Fight for what belongs to you. Forget about technique. Just pound the stuffing out of the next naked-tailed, beady-eyed bully who tries to take away your food."

Chapter 18

W here's my cat?" shouted Amos as he came clumping down the stairs the next morning.

Again Sophia pressed close to Flora while Amos delivered a delicious-smelling mixture of bread and gravy and squash rinds. He cursed as he stuck his bare hand into the bucket and swished the last drops of gravy into Flora's bowl.

"Nothing but rats in Amos's kitchen!" His voice bounced off the sides of the hold. "Hey, cat, I find you, I strangle you myself and feed you to the rats!"

He stomped off.

Flora didn't take her usual few bites of food this time. Instead, she slowly moved until she was standing over her bowl. Sophia stood next to her. After Sophia's pep talk yesterday—and after Sophia agreed to handle the death bites—they decided that today would be all or nothing. Flora even sensed a quietness from the rats, as if they knew a change was coming.

"Watch out!" Sophia whispered.

Flora couldn't see anything. Cats had better eyes in this sort of light than pigs. Then the rat king waddled out of the darkness.

Sophia hissed, and he stopped and sniffed the air. He was clearly more worried about challenging a determined-looking cat than he was about tangling with a pig. He took another step forward.

Sophia hissed again, but the rat simply continued on. Flora felt the old weakness in her knees return.

"Okay, now!" whispered Sophia. "Git 'im!"

Flora's mind went blank. She never did get the hang of Sophia's training. What was she supposed to do? Leap? Claw? Bite?

The rat seemed to smell Flora's fear—he stood up, opened his mouth, and brought his teeth together with a snap.

A flash of anger surged through Flora. How dare this dirty little bully with his dirty little friends demand that she give up her food! Like Nessie from the farm, Flora was fed up, and a mean streak she never knew she had flared. In a flash she spun around, cocked her back foot, and shot it out behind her like a horse.

She felt it connect and heard the rat king land with a soft clink on her discarded chain.

"Yow!" shouted Sophia. "That was perfect!"

Flora turned to look at her enemy stretched out and still. She couldn't believe what she had done. Then the rat's back leg twitched. "Sophia!" she called, not moving her eyes from him. He twitched again. "Sophia, do something. It's killer-instinct time!"

Sophia sprang into action and sank her teeth into the king's neck.

"Here comes another one!" Flora hoped she could do it again.

Sophia let her victim loose and crouched next to Flora. "Make me proud, Deputy!" Every hair on

121 ᘐ

Sophia's back stood on end. The second rat darted close.

Flora spun around. "Pow," she muttered to herself as she lashed out another kick.

The rat tumbled tail over whiskers, and Sophia was on him until he stopped moving. She gave this one a shake before slinking back to Flora's side. "Two down, only two hundred to go!"

Flora circled her bowl, still filled with delicious-smelling food. The thieving mob had crept out from behind the boxes, whiskers quivering. The rats whined and clicked their teeth in frustration. They foamed and twisted over and around themselves, a great surging mass of fur. They weren't looking at the food any longer, they were watching Flora's hind feet.

The rats in front suddenly charged. She spun in place and fired both back hooves at the oncoming furry bodies. Rats tried to climb her and she shook them off, ignoring their sharp claws. Again she lashed out—again and again. Sophia darted around to the stunned ones to deliver bites.

Finally the remaining rats scattered into the shadows, moaning and whining.

"Eight kills!" Sophia leaped into the air and then danced a victory dance. "I did it! I killed a rat! I killed eight rats. I really did it!"

Flora sat, dazed and proud.

"I'm unbelievable!" Sophia crowed. "I'm the queen of cats, the enemy of rats, the sheriff of a

thousand teeth. Beware my killer instinct!" She stood on her hind legs and looked into Flora's eyes. "All that training I gave you sure paid off, *ma chérie,*" she said. "You can thank me later. Come on— let's celebrate. I'm starving."

The two friends had a wonderful feast. Actually, Flora thought she could have eaten a little more, but she was glad to share with the sheriff.

After they were finished, they dragged each rat carcass by the tail over to the stairs, putting them in a neat row. Then they found a corner to curl up in together for an after-battle nap.

What treats would Amos bestow on her now, when he saw what a useful creature his little pig was? Surely he would grant her not just special slops but freedom. She imagined stepping out of the hold and into the sunshine with Sophia, walking down the line of dog cages. Word would have spread about her hidden talent—and she wouldn't be able to hold her head high enough.

Chapter 19

That's more like it!" Amos exclaimed the next morning, staring down at the row of dead rats. Behind the rats sat the sheriff and the larger deputy like two proud fishermen displaying their latest catch. "Rats on my boat got a big problem now!"

Amos nudged one with his toe as if he couldn't believe it was dead. Then he bent down and stroked Sophia's head.

"Good kitty. I make a super choice when I catch you. Champion rat biter!" He chucked Sophia under her chin, which started her purring. She rubbed her side against his leg.

"And you, pig." He turned to Flora. "How did you get off your chain?"

Flora stiffened.

"No, no, no! No pigs walking around. You stay put. You get fat. That's your job." Amos walked over to Flora's chain and stooped to examine the collar. Flora and Sophia followed. "Bad piggy," he muttered to himself.

After filling her bowl with pig slops, Amos reached into his pocket and brought out a length of rope. Looping the rope around Flora's neck, he crafted a collar and clipped it to the chain. Then he tossed the old leather collar away.

Gathering the dead rats by their tails, he climbed the stairs.

Sophia raised her head high. "That is one impressed cook!" She sniffed Flora's slops and turned up her nose. "Don't think I'll need to choke down pig food from now on. I have a feeling Sophia is in line for a special treat. Watch this."

Flora looked at Sophia. Then she looked at her bowl of food that she had worked so hard to protect. Suddenly she didn't feel very hungry.

The door swung open again. This time Amos

carried down a plate of greasy fish and set it in front of the cat. "Good kitty." He petted Sophia on the head. "Strong kitty. Queen kitty. I gotta tell the captain about you!"

When he was gone, Sophia inspected her plate and took a dainty nibble. "Heavenly," she said. "Feels good to get real food delivered right to your feet."

Flora watched Sophia take another bite. "Do you think you can chew through this rope?"

"Hmm." Sophia swallowed and licked her lips. "Could be a problem. Cats don't really chew on ropes. Still, it'll be okay. The rats come to us, remember?"

Flora wasn't comforted.

"Let's eat," said her friend. "We're going to need our strength. They'll be back."

Sophia was right. The rats weren't ready to give up. Or maybe, Flora thought, they let their stomachs do their thinking for them. The first one dashed in on Flora's bowl as Sophia finished her fish.

This time Flora didn't hesitate to fire off kicks. But it was awkward working at the end of the chain, and she didn't feel the same joy inside either.

Still, the rat-extermination team worked their magic over the next few meals. But each day they killed fewer and fewer. The vermin would run off, clicking their teeth and screeching in frustration.

Then it happened. The rats stopped coming.

It would have been comforting to think all of them had been killed. But the sounds of clicks and hisses and chewing remained. Either they'd learned their lesson, Flora thought, or more likely, the two friends had killed off the stupid rats and only the wise and cunning ones were left.

Amos was disturbed when he came down one morning.

"Big problem!" he boomed. He placed the pig slops on the floor and leaned over Sophia. "Lots of alive rats upstairs in my kitchen again. No more dead rats down here where they come from. What's the problem, cat?"

Sophia rubbed herself against his legs, but there wasn't a plate of fish in his hands today. Then she made the mistake of picking out some choice morsels from Flora's slops.

"No!" Amos stomped his foot inches from her tail, making Sophia jump back and hiss. "No more free food for you. You gotta be hungry. Your job is killing rats! No dead rats, no food!"

Amos stayed close while Flora ate her fill. He looked into the shadows from time to time, and when he heard the scurrying of little bodies, he shook his head. Flora was careful to leave a few bites for her friend. But as soon as she stopped eating, Amos picked up her bowl. "No pig food for cats!"

Sophia rubbed herself hopefully on his legs a second time, but he tossed her off.

"Do your job!" he shouted, and stomped up the stairs.

"That was rude," Sophia said, and she began to give herself a thorough tongue bath, as if not knowing where her next meal might come from didn't disturb her.

"*Very* rude," said Flora.

"But it's true." Sophia paused in her licking. "I have to do my job better."

"How?" asked Flora.

Sophia finished her cleaning with a flourish. "Hunt them. Then kill them."

"But how are you going to kill them without me?" Flora pulled against her chain. The rope collar dug into her neck.

"Ha! Sophia doesn't need help. I only needed to get started. I have my killer instinct back. Cat attack! Rat hunting is what cats were made for."

Flora slumped down on her chain.

"Catch you later, pig. Don't run off too far." Sophia nudged Flora on the shoulder. "Just kidding. I'll stop by and say hi if I get a chance between kills. Or when I need a break from hunting."

"Good luck." Flora sighed and then forced a smile. Watching until the little flag of Sophia's tail disappeared into the darkness, she felt more useless than ever.

Chapter 20

For the next few hours, Flora listened to the sounds of the sheriff killing rats. During the silences, she imagined Sophia licking her paw for a moment before going after her next victim.

"Good for you," Flora whispered. She tried to get comfortable and let her mind wander to her real job, the one the captain would give her once they got to their destination.

She laid her head down, and a snowy scene filled her mind. There were no trees, no grass, no stones. There were no creatures—only whiteness. Then over the snow came a sled team with a pig at the lead. A blizzard roared down out of nowhere, until the dogs couldn't see ten feet ahead of them. Their leader didn't need to see. She knew the way by heart. She was unstoppable.

"Don't you give up on me!" she shouted to the dogs behind her. She knew they were exhausted. "Remember this! A sled team is tough. A sled team is strong. We don't give up. And we're a little bit crazy!"

Flora gave a hop and a wiggle to show her boys how unafraid she was, and then she pulled with all her might. The sled surged forward.

Flora slept and dreamed until a new sound woke her up.

It was a cross between a moan and a meow.

Sophia?

The cat queen mewed near Flora's ear. "I can't do it."

She looked terrible. One of her ears was bloody. A patch of fur was missing from her shoulder.

"I'm a failure," she moaned. "Nothing but a hairball. Worthless!"

"What happened?" Flora sat up. "How many rats did you kill?"

"Zero!" Sophia wailed. "They ganged up on me."

Flora couldn't help feeling a tiny quiver of satisfaction. "I wish I could help."

"I shouldn't need help." Sophia threw herself down on the boards. "Cats are supposed to be independent."

Flora tried not to look happy. "You need a team."

Sophia licked her paw mournfully and then looked up. "I do not! I'm a loner."

Flora shook her head to make the chain rattle. "Um . . . maybe you could take a crack at this rope around my neck after all?"

Sophia studied it doubtfully. Then she began to gnaw at the rope. After a few minutes she gave a very uncatlike squeak.

"Did you get it?" asked Flora.

"No," Sophia moaned. "I think I broke a tooth."

Just then something heavy thudded at the top of the stairs, and the door opened with a bang.

"Now I'm gonna teach you a lesson for good!" Amos came into view. In one hand he held Flora's slops, and he had a stick under his arm. With his other hand he dragged a lump that thumped down each step. At the bottom, Amos dropped the lump in a heap.

"You got a new job!" He gave the heap a kick. "I caught you stealing food like a rat. Now you catch rats or you don't eat. Here." Amos threw down the stick. "Bang their heads with this. Lantern and matches are on the stairs."

"I wouldn't have to steal if you fed me enough!" The heap lifted its head.

Aleric!

Amos put the bowl of pig food down and turned back to the boy. "You and that lazy cat had better kill rats every day or you don't eat at all anymore!"

Amos grabbed the bowl when Flora was

finished. "Only the pig eats for free." He stomped
to the top of the stairs and slammed the door.

Flora flinched. She knew she needed her strength.
Still, she hadn't felt good about digging into a bowl
full of food while Sophia and Aleric stood by hungry.

Aleric picked up the stick and pounded on the
stairs. "I won't be treated like a prisoner!"

No answer came from the top.

"He's in worse shape
than I am," whispered
Sophia. "If cats
were the com-
passionate sort, I
would feel sorry
for him."

The boy sat
on the stairs and
put his head on
his knees. Flora
and Sophia waited
and watched. When

they got tired of waiting they curled up together and fell asleep.

Flora woke in the night from Sophia tapping on her nose. Flora sat up. "What's wrong?"

"Shhh. Watch this." Sophia was looking toward a flicker of light moving about in the shadows. "He's hunting."

Sometimes the light would race one way or another, and sometimes the boy's stick could be heard banging against the floor or the walls of the ship.

"He doesn't know what he's doing," whispered Sophia. "You can't hunt rats with a lantern. They'll run and hide."

It was true. Flora could hear rats at the opposite end of the hold scuffling around in the dark. But the boy didn't seem to hear a thing.

The next morning, Amos tromped down with a bowl of food and a scowl on his face. He glared at Aleric, who lifted his head from the bottom of the stairs, where he had spent the night. He kicked at Sophia, who scuttled out of reach of his big boots, but he didn't say a word.

Flora could smell the delicious mixture even before the bowl was set in front of her. The leftovers were still warm. She was hungry as usual, but she wouldn't eat while her companions had nothing. So she stayed where she was and watched Amos's face.

"Pig, eat!" he shouted.

The food smells made Flora's stomach growl and quiver.

"Now everything's wrong on this boat!" Amos hollered. "Rats and thieves eat the food upstairs. The pig doesn't eat food downstairs! I'll never be cook on a boat again."

As he grabbed the bowl away, a great splash of gravy and food slopped onto the floor. Amos paid no attention. Marching up the stairs, he glared at Aleric again. "You kill twenty rats, I give you another chance."

As soon as the door closed, Flora followed her

nose to the spot where the food had spilled. Sophia was already sniffing the edges. When Flora heard clicking, she whispered, "Sophia, stand clear. It sounds like the rats are ready to try again."

Sophia slinked out of sight. A crowd of whiskers and beady eyes appeared in the dim light. Noses twitched as the rats drew closer to the delicious smell.

Flora eased herself into position, ready to bring the hammer down on a rat head. Unfortunately, these were the smart ones. They warily stayed at the edges of the shadows.

After a while, Flora slumped down and pretended to be asleep. She made little snoring noises and watched out of the slits of her eyes.

A trio of rats came out of the shadows and began licking the gravy. Flora trembled with excitement, but she waited. Two more rats joined. Flora jumped to her feet and spun around.

Pow! She let loose and felt her hooves connect with a pair of heads.

Slam! She lashed out again.

Sophia flashed from one twitching body to another. Then Flora and Sophia stood back and looked at their handiwork. Three more.

"Wow!"

Flora turned to see Aleric. He had lit the lantern again. Now he stood gazing at them and the rats. "You guys are amazing! What a team." He reached out and scratched between Flora's ears. It felt heavenly. Sophia didn't even bother to say anything about cats and teams. Instead, she rubbed Aleric's leg.

"Three rats." Aleric stood up. "It's a good start." He reached down again, and Flora thought he was going to give her head another scratch. But instead, she felt his fingers working at the rope around her neck—and felt the weight of the chain disappear.

"Come on, team." Aleric lifted his lantern to show the way. "Let's get to work."

Chapter 21

At first, Flora couldn't see how they could possibly succeed without bait to bring the rats to them. But Aleric led Sophia and Flora behind a wooden post and put his finger to his lips. Then he slipped away.

From the other end of the hold, a terrific banging began along the wall and floor. The knocking and thumping came closer and closer. Soon they could hear the sound of a thousand tiny feet running toward them.

Flora tensed her muscles.

"Turn around and wait for it," Sophia whispered. "I'll tell you as soon as they are in place."

Flora turned.

"Now!" said Sophia.

Flora fired her back feet behind her.

The rats were thrown into a panic. They ran this way and that. Flora kicked and kicked while Sophia dashed in for the cleanup.

As the remaining rats disappeared in the dimness, the lantern bobbed toward them. Aleric fell to his knees, counting in a low voice.

"Nice work. Four more." He laid his stick down and scratched both of his teammates on the head. "What would I do without you guys?"

He tossed the dead rats in a pile, and then he was up again. Flora and Sophia took their places for another round.

By the time Big Amos came downstairs with breakfast, Flora was back on her chain. Sophia and Aleric stood behind twelve rats in two piles, waiting for the cook. Flora looked on with pride. The rats had been hunted down with skill and teamwork.

Big Amos peered at the boy and cat as if trying to understand what had happened. "You two wait for me." After putting Flora's slops out, he went back upstairs and returned with his hands full.

"Good kitty." He put a plate down for Sophia and patted the cat on the head. "Food for rat boy too. Fresh biscuits and scrambled eggs above deck. Come with me and throw these overboard."

Aleric grabbed a bunch of tails in each hand and followed.

He was gone all day, but when he came back with the cook the next morning, he stuck around after Big Amos left. He untied Flora, and all three ran to their places. Flora heard the stick begin knocking at the far end of the ship. She and Sophia smiled at each other and waited for their turn with the rats.

But this time, just as the first wave reached them, heavy footsteps sounded at the top of the stairs. This panicked the rats even more than usual. Instead of simply running from the sound of Aleric's stick, they began leaping about like fish and scurrying in many directions.

Flora felt a split second of fear. What would Amos do if he found her unchained again? But she couldn't waste the work that Aleric had done herding the rats. It was too late to hide anyway.

Her body went into a crouch, and when Sophia gave her the signal, she began spinning and kicking.

When the last of the rats had been killed or had escaped, Flora turned to face Amos.

But it was not the cook.

Standing on the bottom step was another man. He took his hat off and smiled. "I wondered what all that banging was down here. Cook told me some good but mysterious work was being done on our rat problem. I thought I should take a look."

He stepped onto the floor of the hold and walked toward them. "Amos said it was a cat-and-boy operation. But it looks to me as if we have a secret weapon." He scratched behind one of Flora's ears and ran his hand down Sophia's back to the tip of her tail. "If I hadn't seen it for myself, I would not have believed it."

"H-hello, Captain," Aleric stammered.

Flora caught her breath.

"What's your name, son?"

"Aleric, the cabin boy, sir." He brought his feet together and made a clumsy salute.

"Well, Aleric, there is no sailor on this boat working harder than you." The captain clicked his heels and saluted in return. "It seems you have found an unexpected role for the ship's pig. I don't suppose the cook knows about this."

"No, sir." Aleric looked down at the floor. He shuffled his feet. "The pig is supposed to be chained up, getting fat. Please don't tell Cook, sir. I'm in plenty of trouble as it is."

The captain didn't say anything at first. Then a slight smile tugged at his lips.

"Son, you never know who will step up with the brains and talent in a time of need and be the right one for the job. We'll keep this between us—"

Shouting from the deck above interrupted the moment. The captain looked up. "I'd better return to topside. We're closing in on our final destination and we've entered iceberg waters, so we need to be on extra alert. As you can imagine, the precipitation that falls on these coastal areas is significant and can cause a problem with visibility." He laid a hand on Aleric's shoulder. "Carry on, Sailor."

"Yes, sir." Aleric saluted again. "But can I ask you a question, sir?"

"If it's a quick one."

"What happens to me once we reach our final destination?"

"The *Explorer* unloads me and the expedition team, then sails away to pick us up on the other side of the continent. You will be a part of that skeleton ship's crew." The captain gave him a smile. "Meanwhile, the expedition team and I are going by dogsled across the entire span of the Antarctic, something never done before, journeying from food station to food station. If we are successful, we'll have made history."

Flora gazed at him with admiration. Now, there

was a born leader. Something about him reminded her of Oscar.

Aleric jumped in boldly. "I was hoping I could go along on the expedition, sir."

The captain laughed.

Aleric slumped.

"I'm sorry," the captain said. "It's much too dangerous for a boy. Besides, the ship needs every available pair of hands it can get for the difficult trip."

Another shout crackled from the top of the stairs. Loud pounding of boots came from right above them. The captain looked up again.

"More icebergs," he muttered. "I'd better get upstairs. Keep up the good work, son."

But just as the captain stepped on the bottom stair, a bone-numbing jolt knocked Flora off her feet. Her ribs slammed into the floor and knocked the breath out of her. The sound of splintering wood filled the air, and, in a single moment, no one, not even the captain, was in control of anything.

Chapter 22

Flora felt herself skid toward one side of the ship. Barrels and boxes tore loose from their ropes and came tumbling across the hold in the same direction. The crunching sound seemed to go on forever. She came to a stop against a post.

For the tiniest moment, nothing moved. Then the ship slowly righted itself. The men above were shouting to one another, but they sounded far away.

Flora scrambled to her feet. A small stream of water—just a trickle, really—came from nowhere and flowed toward her. She couldn't look at anything else. She just watched the stream as it made its way across the floor.

"Sophia?" Her voice was shaking.

From a corner she saw Aleric stand and run for the stairs.

"Come on!" he shouted.

Flora looked around for her friend. "Sophia!" she squealed. There was no answer.

Instead, the far side of the ship burst open and an icy river washed over her. There was no time to run. No time to scream. No time to even take a breath. The water swept her feet out from under her and carried her, bumping along the floor, until she smacked her head into a floating barrel. It then banged her into the ship's wall and sent her swirling away toward the other side. When her head poked above the waves, she choked and coughed and tried to call out, but the cold water had locked up her lungs.

Now the water began to rise and foam. Flora was not bumping along the floor any longer, and her feet couldn't touch except when her hooves hit underwater boxes. Flora tried to swim to the stairs.

Impossible—the freezing current took her wherever it wished.

She was not the only one struggling. Rats were paddling for their lives all around her. Some tried to climb on her, but the water turned her end for end until she didn't know up from down.

Finally, her hooves touched something solid. She hoped it was the stairs. Her head broke free of the foam, and she gasped for air. The water tried to pull her away again, but she scrabbled and fought to keep her footing. It was the staircase, she was sure. The rats found the same escape route. They swarmed up toward the light and through the open doorway.

Flora struggled to climb onto a dry step. Just then, something grabbed one of her hind legs.

"No!" She desperately tried to pull away. But the thing kept hold of her, tugging her into the seawater once again.

Flora panicked. An octopus must have had one giant arm wrapped around her, taking her under.

Kick, she told herself. *Kick with your other leg!*

She turned her head to aim, but before she could lash out, she saw a face. It was not an octopus. It was the captain. His arm came across her back and held on. His face was gray, as if the water had washed the color from it, but his eyes were clear and questioning.

In answer, Flora focused on getting to the next dry step. It was a good thing she had practiced pulling that big box around the hold. The weight of the captain's body drove her down into a crouch. She straightened her legs slowly and towed her load upward.

But it was no use. The water was rising faster than she was. She could escape the captain's grasp by kicking him off, and in her panic she considered it for a second. Then she gathered her hooves under her and pulled up again and again.

Don't . . . give . . . up.

She was able to climb four or five steps, until the captain's arm slipped off her back. She looked behind her. The man's head rested on a step, and water was already bubbling around his chin. A pair of swimming rats found a toehold in his shirt, scrambled over his shoulders and up the stairs. Flora turned around, took the captain's shirt collar in her teeth, and pulled. The captain lifted his head and helped by pushing with his hands. Step by step, the two of them began to move out of the rising water, but it was still swirling as high as his waist.

Flora felt faint. She couldn't take in air fast enough. Her legs were trembling now from fear, from cold, and from the weight of the captain. She didn't dare let go. She was sure if she did, she would lose him. But she could hardly stand up—and he was starting to slide back.

I'm sorry, she wanted to say. *I failed.*

A shadow fell over her.

Hands reached down to drag the captain up the last few stairs.

Flora let go of his collar and stepped aside. Aleric was not a big person, but by sitting on the top step and heaving his whole body backwards, he was able to slowly haul the captain through the door, onto the deck.

Flora scrambled after them. The sea had almost filled the hold now.

Aleric tried to lift the captain to his feet but failed. "I have the captain!" he shouted over his shoulder. "Don't leave yet!"

Two sailors ran up. Together they lifted the man

up by his feet and shoulders and hurried to where the last lifeboat was bobbing next to the ship's rail. Several men reached out to take the captain into their arms and lay him in the bottom of the boat. The two who had carried the captain followed. Aleric helped Flora into the boat, climbed over the rail, and stumbled aboard last.

They pushed off, and a few men paddled hard with oars to create a distance between the small craft and the ship. Flora looked back when she thought she heard barking coming from the deck, but she couldn't see anything.

As Flora felt the lifeboat find its own rhythm against the waves, the *Explorer* groaned and twisted and tipped over sideways, water streaming down its rounded boards. A wave rose from its roll and clawed at the side of the lifeboat. Flora found her feet knocked out from under her once again, but this time she landed on something soft.

It was the captain. He moaned as Flora struggled off him. She found her footing, climbed onto one of the bench seats, and looked out at the waves.

The *Explorer* was still drifting on its side, sinking lower and lower. Then a puff of air bubbled out as if the ship were breathing its last breath. The men stopped rowing, and everyone turned to watch.

The ship was there one moment, and then suddenly it was not. No big wave followed this time, no white foam, no sign to mark where it had gone down. It was just gone. Bobbing wooden boxes, barrels, and bits of ship parts were all that was left. The iceberg they had struck towered above them like a silent ghost ship, and the men with the oars paddled clear.

Flora shivered; she didn't know if it was from fear or cold.

She spotted a small brown shape floating near their boat. It was a stouthearted rat, paddling hard with its long tail streaming out behind. For the first time, Flora felt sorry for her old enemy. The rat's head was swallowed by a small wave. When it popped back up, it seemed less strong, less brave. Flora knew from her own short swim that no land animal could last long in these freezing waters. When the rat went under again, she quickly looked away.

On board the lifeboat, some men sat with their heads in their hands, and some rowed. No one spoke. Soon they were pushing through a thick soup of ice and ocean. It was hard to see where the sea left off and where the land, if one could call it that, began. Ahead of them another lifeboat was fighting to find a way through, a tiny leaf in rough water. The only sound was the knocking of ice against the sides of the boat.

Wait. Where was Sophia?

Flora looked for a spark of orange in the icy water all around. Had she made it onto the other lifeboat by some chance? Flora didn't see how. The frenzy of the past few moments had been terrible. But the picture in Flora's mind of Sophia fighting the freezing water and going down with the ship was even worse.

Chapter 23

The first thing Flora did when she scrambled off the boat and onto solid ground was to look for her friend. A few dogs had made it to safety. Oscar was one of them.

"Have you seen Sophia?" she asked him through chattering teeth. Oscar was dripping wet and trembling so hard, it looked as if he might shake himself off his feet. He lowered his head but did not answer. A chain, still attached to a broken piece of wood, hung from his neck.

Another dog was more helpful. Flora found out that only he and four other dogs had been released from their chains in time to jump into the first lifeboat. Oscar had been rescued later from the freezing waters. None of the others had survived.

Flora felt like weeping. Cats were not great swimmers. In her bones she knew that her small friend had never had a chance once the water rushed in. Still, she looked around desperately.

Large emergency boxes from both lifeboats were dragged ashore. Tools, dry blankets, and cans of food came out, and when the boxes were empty, the men used axes to chop them up and build a fire. The blankets were laid down around the fire, and a mangy mix of teeth-chattering men and dogs huddled as close to it as they could. Some of the men dashed back out in a lifeboat to see if they could find any more supply boxes or bits of wood in the water. When they had warmed up a bit, others began building walls of snow for a shelter. There was still very little said.

Flora gave up her search and nosed under a corner of a blanket. She now realized how cold she had become. She was shaking harder than she thought possible, but the cold in her bones was nothing compared to the ice in her heart. Sophia could be sharp-tongued and selfish, but without a friend to keep Flora's hope alive all those weeks in the belly of the ship, she didn't know if she would have survived.

Now Sophia was gone.

Rolled up in several blankets, the captain lay on the snow beside the fire, eyes closed. He did not move. Across the fire from Flora, Aleric and Oscar sat, shaking together. The boy had taken Oscar's chain off and was wrapped in a blanket.

Flora was startled to see Aleric's heart beating

inside his blanket. She watched, amazed, as his chest rippled and bumped. Then it popped out!

This was no heart. It was an orange cat with pointy ears, and it looked around with wide eyes. When it saw Flora, it pushed itself free and bounded over to her.

"Sophia!" Flora squealed. Sophia purred and rubbed against Flora. By some miracle, they had both survived. Now that she had a friend and teammate beside her, Flora thought, she could face whatever challenges lay ahead.

When Flora blinked her eyes awake the next morning, the low sun buttered the bumpy snow a light yellow. Boxes that weren't there the night before had been stacked nearby. Sophia's fur tickled her nose from where she was tucked in under Flora's chin.

For a moment, all the fear and sadness from the day before overwhelmed Flora. She felt her heart twist for the brave dogs that didn't make it. Still, here she was—alive with Sophia at her side.

In the night, someone had covered her with a second blanket. The dogs, on the other hand, had moved away from the blankets. They lay in a rough circle in the snow with their noses pointed to the center. Flora imagined they were probably remembering and mourning their lost companions.

As the day continued, Flora watched the men finish the walls of the snow cabin and place one of the lifeboats on top as a roof. They did not sing as they worked. They did not shout or curse or laugh or clomp. Each footstep of their heavy boots landed as softly as a cat's paw.

They carried the captain inside the shelter. Flora had not heard him say a word, but color had returned to his cheeks.

Flora poked her head under her blanket. "Let's go take a look at this place," she said to the fluff of orange. Sophia didn't stir.

Flora brought her head back out and blinked in the sun. The training in the hold had been hard, but

Flora was stronger and more confident now. She was ready to learn new lessons, and she could not ignore her curiosity about the Antarctic.

Sophia's words sounded muffled. "There's nothing to see."

True. The land was white in every direction. Not a plant, not a tree, not any spot of green or brown was visible outside the little camp. Except for a jumble of ice blocks that stuck out of the snow here and there, the terrain was also flat.

"I'm going to go see it anyway." Flora eased out from under the warm blanket, careful not to step on Sophia.

The wind bit into Flora's ribs as she looked first one way and then another. In the distance, a low ridge of mountains rose out of the white. In the other direction, the white took on a light shade of blue where the ice met the sea and bobbed on the waves. She shivered as she remembered floating in the lifeboat out there.

Flora decided to explore a wide circle around camp. The edge of camp felt even colder than the center, and by the time Flora had traveled only half-way, even her teeth were cold. The stiff air froze the insides of her nostrils. There were no smells. This was a land that kept secrets.

Sophia made complaining noises as Flora nosed back under her blanket, bringing in the sharp polar breeze for a moment.

When darkness came, Flora noticed how hungry she was and realized she hadn't seen anyone eating in camp. She snuggled up closer to Sophia for warmth and promised herself that she would not be the first to grumble over something they must all be feeling.

The next morning, the men brought out a large square of material and spread it out next to the snow cabin.

"Is that some kind of special blanket?" Flora asked Oscar.

Oscar took his nose out from under his tail and looked up. "Canvas," he said. "They use it for covering loads or making a shelter."

The edges of the canvas were marked in the snow with shovels, and then it was folded up again. Through the day, the men took turns digging out a rectangle a little smaller than the size of the canvas. All the snow they took out was piled around the perimeter. They chopped and shoveled, piled and patted, until the lowered floor was flat and the snow walls were even, except for an opening with snow stairs going down. Finally they unfolded the canvas, draped it over the walls, pulled it tight, and packed snow on the roof's edges so the canvas would stay put. When the shelter was finished, they moved their tools and supplies inside.

Flora was curious about everything and took quick breaks from her blanket to poke her nose into the new shelter as often as she could without getting stepped on—or noticed by Big Amos. He stayed under the canvas, growling orders to the men about where to stack the supplies that had been salvaged.

None of this activity was of any interest to the dogs, who mostly slept or stretched and then slept some more. But all of that changed when bags filled with frozen fish were carried in. The dogs sat up and sniffed the air. A couple tried to sneak through the doorway but were chased out.

It wasn't long before Amos emerged with his arms full of cans. The men built up the fire again, opened the cans, and put them carefully on the flames. When enough time had passed, they used sticks to lift the hot cans off the fire and sat around eating with their knives. From the smells, Flora could tell they had warmed tomatoes, beans, and chicken soup for their first Antarctic meal.

She was disappointed that none of it was shared with the animals, who watched every bite disappear. Even Sophia poked her head out to look. But the feelings changed to joy when Amos brought over a bag of fish. He opened the bag and began chopping the frozen fish into pieces. The dogs set up a frenzy of barking and whining, but any that came too close got a curse and a kick, and they soon learned that those that sat quietly were fed first.

Flora ate her fish alongside Sophia. It was icy and crunchy and gone in three bites, but it was delicious.

While the animals were eating, the men took a bundle of blankets into the canvas-roofed shelter then disappeared inside the snow cabin next door.

Flora followed the dogs into the shelter and watched them claim sleeping spots. The men had laid the blankets around the perimeter of the shelter. Each dog stood a moment on the spot he had picked and looked around to see if he had a challenger. Then, nose down, each circled three or four times, pawing at the blanket to fluff it up, before sinking into a tight ball and bringing tail over muzzle.

When all six of the dogs were settled inside,

Flora trotted back to where Sophia was trying to keep warm near the dying fire. "Come see what's happening. We need to choose a sleeping spot."

"It won't matter, because it's impossible to get warm anywhere in this place," Sophia complained, but she got up. Against the snow she looked more orange than ever. She hurried across the white ground to the doorway like a cat-shaped sunset.

At the entrance, Sophia stopped and let Flora go in first. Flora hoped the dogs had heard about the job she and Sophia had done on the rats and would accept them as friends. She walked cautiously down the few steps.

As nervous as Flora felt around the dogs, she could only imagine what Sophia was feeling, but the cat bravely made her way to a blanket in the farthest corner. Then she nosed underneath a corner and disappeared. Flora carefully sat on the blanket Sophia had chosen for them and looked around.

Oscar was on the nearest blanket, but except for

raising his eyebrows, he did not move. None of the other dogs seemed to notice the newcomers.

Nose down, Flora began to circle her blanket as she had seen the dogs do.

"Lie down before you step on me," Sophia hissed.

Flora settled down. No one barked. No one made an unfriendly comment. She'd been accepted in the sledding-team home, which already smelled like dog but was surprisingly warm.

Chapter 24

The dogs still didn't seem to have the energy to do anything, but Flora scrambled up with the rising sun—and an empty stomach.

If yesterday's three bites of fish were any indication, they were very low on food. They would have to get it from somewhere else. And they would need sled pullers for the job. She wanted to be one of those pullers.

But as she peered out from the doorway of the shelter, she realized she had not seen any sleds. They must not have made it off the ship! It made Flora sad to imagine the sturdy gliding machines on the floor of the sea. And it made her panic a little to think that even if there was a place to find food, there was no way to get there—or bring anything back.

And when would another ship be heading this way?

Well, Flora wasn't going to let herself sink into gloom. She decided to get used to the cold. She wanted to be ready to work just in case, and what good was a puller with cold feet?

But the moment she stepped outside, the cold became painful. It was the wind that cut the hardest. She nosed into it and felt her nostrils become crusty with frost. Her eyeballs stung. Her breath caught in her lungs, and she couldn't release it without effort. She wondered if her extra hair was doing anything to protect her.

Flora turned her back to the wind. *Don't be a baby,* she told herself. She trotted out and began to make a wide circle in front of the two shelters.

Her knees hurt. *Romp,* she told herself. *Leap about and frisk.* She tried to take a little leap and found that there was no lift in her legs. In fact, she couldn't feel them any longer.

Behind her, she heard a shout and turned. It was Aleric. He looked twice as big in his coat, which seemed to have one or two coats underneath, and he was waving something high in the air. Flora stumbled toward him as best she could, and he knelt down beside her.

Pulling his gloves off, he buttoned her into a dark red coat. He rolled up the sleeves so her front hooves showed. But when she tried to walk, the bottom of the coat dragged on the ground. She couldn't avoid stepping into it.

Aleric shook his head. "It's too big. Wait right here."

He returned with a knife and a length of rope, then helped Flora out of the coat. After he cut a wide strip off the bottom, he buttoned her back into the coat and cinched it around her middle with the rope. She looked back and tried to see herself. She was sure she looked funny.

She took a few steps and stopped. Her coat whispered with every move, but no part dragged on the ground, and she felt so cozy. Even her eyeballs felt warmer.

When Sophia woke up, she made a surprised sound and walked around Flora slowly, then woke up Oscar to look. They sat together and stared.

Oscar cleared his throat. "I wondered how you were going to make it out here. This answers one of my biggest questions."

Sophia nodded. "I don't have to worry about my bed partner turning into a pigsicle any longer."

Flora stepped back out into the pale light.

She began to run around the camp.

She pushed hard until the cold air burned her throat. Then she ran even more.

The lifelessness of the land still amazed her. There were no seals or polar bears or rabbits disappearing into their holes. No mice or birds, not even a single seagull.

"I sure wouldn't mind if there was a little color

173

out there," she said to one of the other dogs when she returned to the shelter.

The dog's eyes twitched as if he were surprised to be spoken to, but he didn't respond.

She tried again. "Even a spot of green poking up out of the snow would do my heart good."

The dog gave a big sigh and turned his nose in under his tail.

Flora looked around the cave. "But one thing's for sure," she said in a louder voice. "A little run around camp loosens your lungs and makes breathing easier."

It was as if she weren't there. No one even turned to look at who was talking. Even Oscar and Sophia were ignoring her, curled up together sleeping.

One morning, after Flora came back inside from a romp, she heard a dog telling the others that the men were having a meeting.

Flora leaned over to Oscar. "We should have a meeting too," she said.

Sophia moved to her side, and Oscar came closer. "Plans are afoot," he said.

Flora's heart thrilled. She was pretty sure that any plans would involve pulling something, even if there were no sleds.

"Huff!" Oscar suddenly lifted his head and crossed his eyes in an effort to look down his nose. A hair was stuck to one of his nostrils. He huffed again, and the hair took flight, fluttering down to the blanket. "Cat hair," he muttered.

"At least it doesn't smell like a dog," Sophia said.

Flora coughed politely and sat down. "You said there were plans afoot. What happens to the expedition now?"

"No dogsleds," said Oscar. "No expedition."

"Couldn't they send a replacement ship with a new sled?"

"No ship," said Oscar. "No replacement, no expedition. There is a new project now, and it is called staying alive as long as possible. We might be lucky and get rescued, or the men might try to sail away in the lifeboats and save themselves. That's probably what they're meeting about."

Sophia was quiet, but Flora knew she was listening.

"No matter what, it means the food has to last a long, long time."

Flora nodded. The once-a-day fish feedings had gotten even smaller.

Oscar went on. "Actually, there is more food, out in the snow."

Flora stopped herself from jumping up. She remembered Oscar talking about this, but it didn't seem important before.

"About four months ago, the captain brought a different crew and two dog teams, including me, to the Antarctic. We landed not more than a mile from here. Each team pulled big boxes of food on sleds to two separate food stations out there." Oscar pointed his nose to the snowy wilderness. "We did that so those on the final expedition wouldn't have to carry so much food with them. The first food station is at least three days from here—"

"But we don't have a sled to bring back the supplies," Flora finished.

Sophia's tail twitched. "Let's not get too worried. We should know a lot more as soon as the men finish their meeting."

"Um . . . yup," Oscar muttered. "I'm a little tired. Better take a nap."

Outside, there were shouts and the sound of work being done. Flora walked to the doorway and saw men moving about with a new sense of purpose.

The extra lifeboat, with canned food already loaded inside, had been set down on its belly as if it were about to sail away on the snow. Ropes, tied to the front, lay stretched out, ready for pullers.

Wow. She had to tell Oscar about this. The dogs were sniffing and talking to one another in low voices.

Aleric was in a terrible mood as he helped carry cans. "I didn't sign on to this crew to be a nursmaid," he complained out loud. No one was listening, but that didn't stop him. "I don't know anything about taking care of a broken leg and busted ribs. Why do I have to stay in this nowhere place?"

Flora didn't have to go tell Oscar. He slipped by her and sidled up beside the boat, pacing and looking more excited than she had seen him in a long time.

"Oscar." She ran up to him. "They're going to use the boat as a sled, aren't they? They're going to go get the food, right?"

"Nope." Oscar didn't seem to be able to stop walking and sniffing. "They decided to pull the boat to a place where they can safely put it in the water, sail off, and flag down a passing ship to come rescue the captain and a few others who have to stay in camp, poor bums."

Flora wanted to do a crazy dance. Pulling! It was about to start!

Big Amos had made a sort of table in front of the men's cabin out of wooden boxes. He was sharpening his knives. When Flora walked by, he got very excited and dropped to his knees at the doorway. "Come to me, my little sausage!"

Flora backed away hastily, but she wasn't fast enough. His hands ran inside her coat over her sides and legs.

"Oh, not so fat now. No worry. Still a nice pig. You come back same place tomorrow."

Tomorrow, she hoped, she'd be out doing her job far away from him.

Chapter 25

That night, Flora was awakened by a small furry paw tapping her ear.

"Get up," whispered Sophia.

Was it time to get hitched to the boat already? Flora rose immediately and silently followed Sophia out of the cave.

Someone else was outside too. It was Oscar. A light snow was falling.

"Come on." Oscar sniffed the air. "We have a lot to do tonight."

Finally, a pulling adventure! Flora's heart soared as they crept through the camp. She noticed the packed-up makeshift sled. They were awake even earlier than the rescue crew.

"Where are we going?" she asked.

No one answered. She followed the two dark shapes in front of her. They seemed to know what they were doing. The falling snow had turned into tiny ice pellets that made a hissing sound on the ground and a patter on her coat. The cold began seeping into her body, but Flora was determined not to complain.

It was strange to see Sophia outside of the cave. Her soft feet seemed to float above the surface of the snow.

"Where are we going?" Flora asked again.

Oscar stopped to listen and sniff the air.

"We're trying to find the right place." Sophia sat and chewed some ice from between her paws. "And trust me, this isn't it!"

Oscar shook himself, sending out a spray of ice. Flora had to close her eyes as pellets bounced off her snout.

"Hey," said Sophia. "Thanks a lot. We have enough ice falling out of the sky without your throwing more in our faces."

"Sorry," Oscar mumbled, and started moving.

Flora trotted behind her friend and thought again about how unusual it was to see Sophia outside, away from her blanket.

"Did you say 'the right place'?" asked Flora. "The right place for what?"

"For you." Oscar didn't stop this time.

"Oh." Flora looked around. She couldn't see how one place in all this flat whiteness was any different from another place—or different from camp.

"You're getting behind," called Sophia. "Hurry up."

Flora hustled. "Why do I need a place?"

The only answer was the hiss of sleet on snow.

She tried to puzzle it out. Oscar wouldn't bring them out in the cold at night unless this was important. And Sophia wouldn't be out unless . . . Flora couldn't imagine what would make Sophia take a walk on a night like this.

Oh, wait. Of course.

Oscar was sick. That was it. Oscar was too sick to pull the boat sled, and Sophia must have agreed to help prepare Flora to take his spot. Someone would have to be trained to handle the lead-dog duties. They wanted to do this away from the others, where Oscar wouldn't be embarrassed.

Flora felt a shimmy rising up in her and quickly pushed it down. She felt like kicking and prancing, but she kept walking. This was serious business. She couldn't let her friends know she suspected anything. They must have been working this out during her morning romps.

Maybe every sled dog, or sled puller, had to go through special training. And lead dogs probably had the toughest preparation of all. With growing excitement, Flora imagined herself in the lead position. She hoped the other dogs wouldn't be too upset that they weren't chosen. She'd have to be careful to appear humble and respectful of her less-qualified brothers.

Oscar looked around and gave her an encouraging nod.

Flora felt dizzy. She put her head down and concentrated on walking. She was up for this. She wouldn't disappoint them.

Chapter 26

Finally they stopped. When Flora looked behind her, she couldn't see the camp any longer and their tracks were being covered by sleet.

Oscar scratched around until he found a soft place in the snow. "I'll start digging here."

"Is this the special place?" asked Flora.

Sophia looked uncomfortable. The falling sleet made her blink. She started to say something but then began licking her front instead.

"It's okay," said Flora. She wanted to make this easier on her friend. "My strength has been tested before. I've been working up to this moment. I think I'm ready."

Sophia looked relieved. "Good. You're going to

have to stay away from camp in this one-pig home for a few days."

Alone? A tiny stab of fear pricked Flora's heart. Staying in a hole reminded her of being down in the hold. This might be harder than she thought.

Oscar dug away at the hole with short, expert strokes.

"Should Oscar be digging that hard?" Flora asked.

"He'll be fine. He's hurrying because he's looking forward to leaving with his team," Sophia said. "But don't worry. I'll remember the way back here."

Flora shivered inside her coat. The cold felt as if it were squeezing her brain. This didn't make sense. An icy breeze sprang up and whisked her breath away in long white streams. She shook her head, trying to shake out the confusion.

Oscar's head was out of sight now. Plumes of powder shot from the hole.

Flora shook her head again, this time with worry for Oscar.

"He's sick," she said, hoping this didn't hurt the dog's feelings. "I can help."

"I'm not sick." Breathing heavily, Oscar backed his head out of the hole, his sides heaving from the effort. "I'll be fine. Digging is good for dogs. It's like medicine."

"Oscar needs to dig fast," Sophia said, "if he wants to get back to camp before they leave."

Flora stamped the snow. The crust broke under her feet, and she sank up to her ankles. "I don't understand."

Sophia went on as if Flora hadn't spoken. "Remember, the new project is all about staying alive. Oscar's job is to lead the rescue crew. Your job is to keep out of sight for a while."

What kind of job was that? If this special place wasn't for training, then what?

"Do I stink? Is that the problem?" Flora sniffed herself. Her hair smelled a little bit like dog from spending nights in the snow shelter, but that was hardly her fault.

Oscar huffed and started digging again.

Flora went on. "Everybody says pigs stink, but I have clean habits even if I don't lick myself all the time."

"You don't stink," said Sophia. "Do you think I would curl up next to you every night if you were a stinky pig? I'll come back after the dogs have gone."

"What? What are you talking about? Oscar, stop ignoring me." Flora's voice trembled now, but she didn't care.

If he could hear her with his head inside the hole, he didn't show it.

"Stop digging!" she shouted into the wind. She moved to stop Oscar.

Sophia stepped in front of Flora. "Oscar is saving your life," she said. "Don't you understand? You're in terrible danger."

Flora sat down with a thump in the snow. "I'm in danger?"

Oscar backed up and out of the hole to catch his breath.

Flora continued, "I don't need a special place. For a sled pig, having an adventure is like medicine."

Sophia gave her a pitying look. "They didn't bring you along to be a sled pig."

"They didn't?" Flora looked at Oscar.

"Nope." He shook his head.

"If you're saying that because you're sick, and you're afraid I'll take over your lead-dog spot . . ." Flora faltered and then went on. "You should know you don't have to worry. I won't."

Oscar turned back to the hole. "I'll clean out the last little bit. It's almost ready."

Flora jumped up. "Why won't someone just say what's going on?"

"Calm down," said Sophia. "He's digging you a hiding place. A new home for a little while until the danger is past."

"But I want us to face the danger together. Like a team."

Sophia glared at Flora. "I don't need a team,

remember? And I'm cold and wet. This business of trying to keep others safe is starting to put my whiskers in a knot."

Flora paced in an angry circle, churning up the ice and snow under her feet. She paid no attention to the sharp edges nicking her legs. It was just like Sophia to forget how she had needed help with the rats.

"I haven't been any trouble." Flora stopped pacing. "Wait a minute. Are you two trying to get rid of me?"

Oscar cleared his throat as if he wanted to say something but panted instead.

Yes, she understood now. "You're afraid of me, both of you. You know I'm strong, and you think I'll take all the credit. Well, I can see through your plan, and I have another plan. Goodbye!"

Flora marched off with her head high in the air. Oscar's voice floated through the wind to her. "Where are you going?"

"Back to camp," Flora answered without turning around. Then she realized she had no idea which direction camp was. She stopped and cast her head back and forth, trying to remember. Nothing was familiar, and everything was familiar. All the land looked the same—just plain white.

She turned and walked back to the dog and cat, who were still watching her. "I decided to give you a chance to follow me."

Sophia's tail swished impatiently in the snow. "A sled dog would never lose his way back home."

Flora looked at Oscar, who blinked and shifted his feet.

"A sled dog has an unfailing sense of direction," said Sophia. "He has broad shoulders for pulling, and he has big, padded feet, which don't break through the crust."

Flora looked at the ground where her hooves had chopped up the snow and ice. She felt miserable, lost, and terribly lonely, even though she was not yet alone. "Let's pretend you're right for a minute. Why would they have brought me along if it wasn't to be a sled pig?"

Sophia shook snow off her shoulder. "I didn't want to tell you because I thought you would figure it out for yourself."

Figure it out.

The wind seemed to stop for a moment, and silence filled Flora's ears.

"Food," said Sophia.

Chapter 27

Flora's head felt light. She felt sick and wanted to lie down. She sat with a thud.

Oscar sighed. "Pulling is for dogs."

"Do you think Amos likes you because of your personality? Think about it," said Sophia. "They want you on their adventure, all right. But not for the reason you think."

"No," Flora whispered. But the signs were all there. She had a purpose on this expedition, and it had nothing to do with how smart she was or how brave or strong.

She was food.

Oscar turned and sniffed at the hole he had finished. He gave the piled snow at the entrance a swipe. "I think it's big enough now."

Flora stood up and backed into it. Her ears were ringing, and she barely noticed when her friends said goodbye. Sophia stopped once and looked back, but it had begun to snow and they were soon out of sight.

Flora slid in deeper and curled up. She found that her back legs could tuck inside the bottom of her coat. Her hole was warm as could be.

She shivered anyway.

The snowflakes slowly filled in the opening as if filling in a grave.

Chapter 28

For two snowy days Flora lay in her little cave. When she got thirsty, she ate snow. When she got hungry, she struggled up through the powder and walked around until the feeling eased, being careful never to lose sight of her frozen home.

Cold white emptiness was everywhere, and it pulled the hope from her heart.

Don't . . . give . . . up.

This time the words didn't work.

Flora tried to find a memory from her piglet days on the farm—a thought or a picture that could be a source of warmth to melt the ice in her mind.

Luna. Flora worked hard to remember everything about her old friend—her face, the way she held her tail, the color of her fur, the sound of her voice—and a warm light came. Flora could almost hear their conversations about dogs and stars and even the ocean. Luna seemed to know so much about life . . .

Flora's thoughts froze. She tried *not* to think. Yet she couldn't stop the truth from crowding in.

Luna knew all that time how Flora would end up.

I'm a fool. A big, fat fool. Well, not fat, really. At least not anymore.

This was a cruel world she had been born into, all pink and squirming. She'd never wanted to see reality. Now, like the cold, it was impossible to ignore.

She curled into a tight ball.

At the end of two days, Flora had to fight a growing feeling of panic.

By now Oscar would be off with the dog team.

And she was sure Sophia had tried to figure out the way back to her and couldn't.

Her thoughts turned darker.

Perhaps she had been left here to die. Probably her friends had chosen this fate for her—starvation versus the knife. Flora wasn't sure which she would have chosen, but she didn't like someone else choosing for her.

Then she thought she heard Sophia calling her name. It sounded like a voice from a dream. Flora wanted to jump up and shake off her snow hole like a dirty blanket. She wanted to race out and be found.

But things were different now. She was food. She had to be looked after, protected like a baby. She was a burden, not a team member.

She pushed her head through her thin roof. Oscar was there. He was sniffing around in circles. Sophia was sitting and calling.

When Oscar saw her, he came running up and licked her chin. Sophia ran a few steps too, but then, catching herself, slowed to a dignified walk.

Flora stumbled out on legs that felt stiff and wooden. She nosed the cat in the ribs. She had to admit she was delighted to see her friends again. But she didn't want to be delighted.

"I see you're still alive." Sophia gave in to acting like a kitten and batted Flora's cheek with a paw.

"It wasn't too bad." This huge lie was the only thing Flora could think to say.

"We would have come back sooner if it was possible," said Sophia. "It's safe now. Amos is gone."

Flora changed the subject. "What are you still doing here, Oscar? I thought you would be out pulling."

Oscar looked to the horizon and didn't answer.

"They wouldn't take him," Sophia said softly. "He tried. He stood in the lead spot when it was time to get in the harness, but they wouldn't hook him up. Smart if you ask me. He's not well."

"Pulling is like medicine," said Oscar. "You wouldn't understand."

Flora winced. Poor Oscar.

"He was almost as upset as Aleric," said Sophia. "They both got left behind."

As Oscar led them back to camp, Sophia continued on about how Amos had screamed and waved his knives at everyone until the whole camp was out searching for Flora, and how he had tried to use the dogs to track his escaped pig.

"Oscar thought ahead, though." Sophia glanced at Oscar. "He dragged the search team in one wrong direction after another. Of course they never even got close to your hiding place."

Flora wanted to smile. She wanted to dance around and laugh at the image of Big Amos thundering about in the wrong places. But she felt empty—hollowed out.

"They finally had to give up," Sophia said. "Amos and the other men finished loading and hooked up the dogs. Off they went to get help. Only the captain and the sailor with the broken leg stayed behind with Aleric."

"Why didn't they take the captain?" asked Flora.

"Too sick to travel." Oscar looked back at them to answer. "And weight. Sled dogs are strong, but every pound counts. There weren't enough of us . . . of them to do the job. I could have pulled, though. They needed me. Pulling is like medicine for a sled dog." He hung his head.

"You said that already," said Sophia.

"Well, it's true."

Sophia caught Flora's eye and shook her head.

Twice on the walk back, Flora noticed Oscar breathing extra hard. Something rattled in his throat whenever he got winded. Sophia would pretend to be tired and need a rest, and they would all stop until Oscar looked able to go on.

It was during the stops that Flora noticed how hungry she was—hungry enough to eat a boot, laces and all.

"Where were the men and dogs going?" she asked. "Did they change their minds and head for the food station?"

"No, they're going north," said Oscar. "Anywhere there might be people. They'll put to sea when they find a good place. If they can find help, they'll come back the same way, I expect. If they don't find help . . ."

Flora knew how that sentence ended.

If they came back without finding help, they'd think again about killing the pig.

Chapter 29

Aleric was the only one outside when they came into camp.

"Hey, the pig is back!" he called.

A limping sailor hobbling on a wooden stick came to the door of the snow cabin. Flora didn't like the way he looked at her.

She would be keeping far away from that one.

Aleric put out three small frozen fish that Flora attacked. She looked up to see Sophia and Oscar watching. She felt a little ashamed but still couldn't help licking the snow where the fish had been. It was her first meal in three days, and she felt almost as hungry as before.

Aleric scratched her behind the ears. "I wish I

could give you more." His fingers moved under her chin. "I never met an animal with better timing than you when it comes to killing rats and not getting killed yourself. You are one smart pig. Now we all need to figure out how you and the rest of us can stay alive until they come back."

Flora glanced at the sailor with the stick.

Men and animals all slept in the snow shelter together now. The nights were getting colder. The snow shelter was smaller and kept the warmth better than the drafty cabin with a lifeboat as the roof.

Most of the boxes were gone, along with the other dogs, so there was plenty of room.

Aleric had made beds for the men by layering several blankets for padding. The captain spent all his time in his bed, for he was still weak and spoke very little. Flora decided she'd curl up against him at night to keep him warm. It was an easy job.

Flora's knowledge about her role on the expedition was not the only thing that had changed during her time in the hole. She didn't feel the cold as she had before either. After those two days on her own, her body was able to handle the freezing temperatures. She could now stand being outside for several hours each day. She still kept up her trot around the camp—partly out of habit and partly so she'd be fit to run if the sailor ever got close.

But the biggest change in Flora was that she no longer dreamed of dogsledding. She dreamed only about food. She was always hungry.

One morning, Flora heard the sound of pounding. She gently pulled herself away from the captain's side and walked to the doorway. Aleric had found a hammer, saw, and nails. He was taking loose boards from wooden crates and making them into a box. Then he dragged the lifeboat off the top of the empty cabin and banged on it until it fell apart.

He laid out two curved pieces from the front of the boat parallel to each other like sled runners. He placed straight boards across both runners, nailed them down tight, and then attached the wooden box he had made.

"What does he think he's doing?" Sophia had stepped up beside her.

"It's a homemade sled," said Flora.

They watched Aleric tie a rope to the front of the box. He made a loop in the free end. Then Flora heard the captain's voice calling.

Aleric ducked past them into the snow shelter. In a few moments he reappeared, pulling the captain on a blanket. The captain's eyes were brighter, and Flora thought he appeared to have regained some of his strength. Aleric helped him sit up with his back against the wall of the shelter so he could see.

But it was Oscar who took the most interest in the project. After so many days of rest, he seemed to be feeling much better. He sniffed the loop at the front of the sled, walked around the whole thing, and then stayed close to Aleric's side, even getting underfoot at times, especially when Aleric bent to pick up the loop.

A spark of Flora's old feelings flickered to life.

She tried not to remember. She tried not to feel. *Stop it,* she told herself.

But her desire to run with a team—to come through when everyone was counting on her, maybe even have a crack at leading the pack—wouldn't go away. The truth was Flora wanted to walk—no, dance—around the whole sled herself.

Fiercely, she pushed away these thoughts. She

crawled back into the snow shelter, into the darkest corner, and spent the rest of the day alone.

But that night in her dream she flew high above the earth in a moonless sky. Behind her, like a falling star, sailed a silver sled.

Chapter 30

That sled you're building is more than just a toy, isn't it?" It was the captain's voice. Aleric and the two men were sitting on their beds.

Flora looked around. Where were Oscar and Sophia? She inched toward the door.

"I hate being hungry all the time. And if the others don't make it back . . ." Aleric had a hammer in his hand. He began scraping at the floor of the snow shelter with the claw end but then stopped and tamped the loose snow back into place. "You said there was a food station three days out and that it's not needed now for the expedition. I'd like to go find it and bring supplies back."

"Well, by now you probably know how to use the sun and stars to navigate from watching the crew," the captain said. "And of course the dog has already been there. These sled dogs have an amazing ability to remember their way back to a place they've already visited, and Oscar is one of the best. But even for me, with all of my experience, it's extremely dangerous, even reckless, to head into that inhospitable terrain alone. Besides, I'm not convinced the dog is well enough to pull. It'll be a heavy load when the supplies are added."

"But Oscar looks almost like his old self." Aleric thumped the side of his boot with the hammer.

The captain hesitated. "Let's discuss this again in a few days. My health has been improving steadily. I should be the one to make the journey."

Flora shook her head. Oscar was looking much better, but he was hardly back to his old self, and the captain would be lucky if he could even stand without help in a few days.

"We don't need more food." The sailor poked his stick into the snowy floor. "Why don't we just eat the pig?"

Flora felt the hairs on her neck stand up. She measured the remaining distance to the door. She could make a run for it if the sailor got any ideas about jumping on her.

"That pig saved my life." It was the captain.

"Well, it could save your life again, Captain, and I know just the recipe."

The captain did not answer. Flora slipped out and walked until the camp was barely visible. She wished she could just keep walking. She was so tired of being afraid.

Later that morning, the captain was dragged out to his place against the shelter.

"Tell me if you see something that will make this thing glide better," Aleric said to him. Then, looping the rope over his neck and under one shoulder, he gave the new sled a pull. Oscar followed, woofing. When Aleric didn't stop, Oscar ran in front and almost tripped the boy until Aleric took the loop off and placed it around Oscar.

The big dog now walked like a king, pulling

the sled with his head high. About ten steps later, the loop slipped off his chest and down to the snow. Oscar picked it up in his teeth and dragged the sled another few steps, making everyone laugh.

Flora couldn't help but smile too.

"I feel better already." Oscar flopped down beside her. He looked better, although he was breathing hard. "Pulling is like . . ."

"Medicine." Flora finished. "I know—you told me already."

"Yup," said Oscar. "And I've been needing a dose of that medicine for a long time."

After a quick rest, Aleric brought out a second

rope. Flora's heart jumped. But he tied the new rope to the sled and made a loop for himself. He adjusted Oscar's rope so it wouldn't slip off. Together they pulled the sled in a tight circle as a team.

Flora couldn't stand it any longer. She trudged away again, this time far into the white until the sounds from camp faded. She looked all around. It was so strange to feel trapped in the middle of so much open space. But that was exactly how she felt.

When she finally followed her tracks back, the sled was gone and so was everyone else except the captain. He had fallen asleep sitting up. Flora lay down at his side.

They both woke to a loud whooping. The sled seemed to be returning from a trial run. Sophia hopped off as they came to a stop and batted playfully at Oscar, who was pulling the sled by himself. Aleric had made him a sort of harness out of smaller ropes. Oscar looked happy but tired.

Aleric helped the sailor stand up from where he

had been sitting in the bottom of the box and then unhooked Oscar.

"Sir." Aleric walked up to the captain and saluted. "We've practiced with extra weight in the sled, a fully grown man plus me, and the dog did fine. I know you wanted more time to consider, but we don't have time. I'd like permission to go out in search of the food stores."

The captain looked at his boots.

Oscar joined the boy and Aleric reached down and patted him on the ribs. "I have the strength to help Oscar pull if need be. But I'm not getting any stronger on the little bit of food we get each day."

The captain shook his head. "My mind is made up. It's no job for a boy alone. We'll devise a plan in a few days."

Aleric crossed his arms. He looked bigger and more confident than the boy Flora had met that first day on the dock.

"I know I'm only a cabin boy. But you were the

one who said you never know where brains and talent will come from. It might be time to find out."

"No." The captain's voice was kind but firm. "Permission denied. I would be sending you to your doom."

"Yes, sir."

Flora was surprised at how easily Aleric seemed to give up.

The boy looked around at the fading light. "It's time to get inside, sir, and have a bite to eat. It's too cold for you out here." Aleric covered the captain's legs with the blanket and gently pulled him into the snow shelter.

After Aleric dished out the evening meal, he tucked more blankets around the captain while everyone got ready for bed. Flora lay down again at the captain's side.

"Keep him warm, pig," said Aleric.

Flora woke in the middle of the night. She listened for the sound that had awakened her, but all was silent. She raised her nose to sniff the air and then cocked her head and listened again. The captain was breathing slow and steady. The sailor was snoring loudly. But something was different.

Aleric and Oscar were missing, and so was Sophia.

Flora stepped outside quietly so as to not wake anyone. She looked around in the half-light. The sled was gone, but the runners had made clear marks in the snow, disappearing in a straight line into the great wilderness.

Flora knew this was no practice run. No matter what the captain had said, Aleric and Oscar and Sophia were off on their brave quest, and they had left Flora behind.

Chapter 31

They're gone."

Flora jumped. Sophia had come up behind her silently. Flora turned back to look at the tracks. "I figured you were with them."

"I wasn't invited." Sophia stepped forward and cleaned an ear with a paw. She sneezed and shook her head. "Oh well. Why would a cat want to go on a journey where she could end up dead, and all for the sake of others?" She paused. "Still, I can't help being worried about Oscar. He acts like he's better, but I think he's still sick."

"He *is* still sick, and I'm going after them." Flora's own words surprised her. She hadn't known she was going to say them, but she knew they were exactly right.

"No, you're not. You'll never make it out there. You weren't made for South Pole adventures."

Flora gave her an icy look. "I think I know by now what I was made for."

"If you stay here, we have a good chance of getting rescued," said Sophia.

"Getting rescued is good," said Flora, "if you're a cat." She stepped in between the sled tracks. "Like you said, no one can resist a cat. But pigs don't get rescued. They get fattened up for later."

Sophia followed, rubbing her side on Flora's hind leg. "Aren't you afraid of dying out there?"

"Nope," said Flora. "I'm afraid of being afraid for the rest of my life. Well, best of luck and happy rescues." She took a few steps.

"You'll regret this decision." Sophia jumped in front of Flora.

Flora stepped around her friend. "Maybe. But I think the captain is right. Oscar and Aleric aren't in good enough shape to make it on their own. I believe I can pull a sled as well as any dog."

"Speaking of the captain, what about him? He needs you."

"He needs the food that will be coming on that sled even more."

Sophia looked back at the camp, but when Flora trotted off again, the cat dropped in behind and stayed at her heels.

Finally Flora spun around in a cloud of powder. "What are you doing?"

Sophia shook the snow off her ears. "You're not the only one who can be stubborn."

Flora felt a shiver in her knees, and it wasn't from cold. It was a shiver of hope that she'd have a teammate and not be alone in the emptiness. That was selfish, though. Out there was no place for a cat. "You're hardly bigger than a snowball. You'd just be a burden."

"At least I don't sink into the snow up to my knees with each step," said Sophia.

"Go home, snowball."

"I'm not going to stay at camp and be . . . alone. It doesn't work for me anymore."

"Then you're a fool."

"I used to be a fool," said Sophia. "A stubborn fool. I didn't know enough to stand by my friends. Now I'm just stubborn. Look, we've got a long way to go. If the pigs among us can manage to stop being so hardheaded and independent, it will be a lot easier on the cats."

"I can't believe a cat is lecturing a pig on being too independent." Flora started out again with Sophia right behind.

Despite what Sophia said about her hooves, Flora didn't break through the icy crust. She clipped along easily. Besides the swishing of her coat and the tapping of her hooves, there was nothing else to hear. Sophia followed on such silent feet that Flora had to turn her head to see she wasn't alone. That was when she noticed the camp had disappeared from sight behind them.

"I hope you know how to take care of yourself, Sheriff," she said from the front, "because I don't know how to take care of either one of us."

The two animals kept up their easy trot at first. But by late afternoon, the sled tracks led into an ice field that looked as if someone had chopped into it with a giant ax. Great big chunks of ice were standing on end. The sled tracks weaved in and out and over these frozen boulders.

Flora stopped, and Sophia came up alongside. The wind had picked up, blowing ice pellets sideways in little white waves.

"I wonder if we should press on or stop here for the night." Flora pretended to think about these words, but she was watching Sophia out of the corner of her eye. She hoped Sophia, with her practical nature, might have an idea.

But Sophia was watching Flora.

Finally Flora couldn't help herself. "Did Oscar teach you any tricks about staying alive out here?"

"If he did, I wasn't paying attention."

"I think I missed that lesson myself."

Sophia looked back the way they had come.

It was starting to get too dark to travel. Flora walked forward a few steps and found herself out of the wind behind a large ice boulder. She began to hollow out a spot to spend the night. Her hooves were not as good as Oscar's paws at digging snow, but she managed to make a rather shallow nest. Sophia made her own nearby but ended up between Flora's front feet.

It was a cold sleep that night, interrupted often by the howling wind. No dreams came. Flora breathed in Sophia's smell and wondered how Oscar was doing pulling the sled.

Hang on, she wished she could tell him. *We're coming.*

Chapter 32

We've lost our trail!" Sophia called out the next morning. "Last night's wind must have blown it away. But we can still turn back."

She had climbed a tall ice pillar and was looking at the tracks leading back to camp, which were deeper and somewhat visible.

Flora tried not to show the panic in her heart as she stretched and sniffed around for a clue. Surely they weren't defeated after just one day. "Turn back, then. I want to find that crazy, sick dog and the boy who won't listen to his captain."

"If I turn around, you'd better stick with me, pig. You couldn't find an iceberg if you were standing on it."

"I could if I had a friend who told me to look

down!" She looked up at Sophia and noticed something. The block of ice Sophia was standing on had been scraped. There was a line at about the height of Flora's head, as well as another mark at the same height a little farther away.

"Tracks!" she called up.

"You're looking in the wrong place. Tracks are on the ground."

"Aleric's not the most experienced driver. I think the sides of the sled might have bumped into the chunks of ice here and there. See if you can spot any more scrapes.

Sophia gazed in the direction Flora was looking and then hopped down. "You're right for once. From up there I can tell which direction they were heading."

Flora grinned. "Then let's keep moving, cat. I found the iceberg. Now you find our friends."

Sophia stepped into the lead, occasionally leaping to the top of an ice mound to check her course.

Two hours later, they found the spot where

Oscar and Aleric had spent the night. Aleric had made a small fire, and a few bits of charcoal could be seen in the snow. They were almost through the field of giant broken ice by now. Sophia climbed to the top of one last pillar.

"Flat country ahead!" she shouted. "And clear tracks again. Pick up the pace, slowpoke."

Flora was so happy to hear the good news, she didn't bother to respond to the insult. She started clipping along a little faster, and soon she could see the flat plain herself. Apparently the wind and sleet hadn't blown through there during the night.

However, they were up on a ridge, and to get to the plain below, she and Sophia would have to find a way down a long slope of sheer ice.

There was no snow on it at all. Anything on the ice simply slid to the bottom. Flora could see the scrapes where Aleric must have tried to drag his boots to slow the sled down. The scrapes led to a hole and a lot of churned-up snow at the bottom, where the sled had probably crashed and had then been pulled out.

Sophia walked a few steps down the slope and was able to keep her footing.

"Come on!" she called.

Flora stepped out as gingerly as possible. But in an instant her feet splayed in four directions and she was on her belly, sliding helplessly. No amount of scrabbling could stop her.

She plowed into her traveling companion, knocking Sophia's feet out from under her. Sophia yelped and tried to stop herself with her claws, but Flora's weight carried the two of them down like polished stones.

They struck the soft snow at the bottom with a *plop* close to where Aleric's sled had landed. Snow went up Flora's nose, and she sneezed.

"Get off me!" Sophia yowled, and struck out with her claws to make the point.

Flora squealed and struggled to find her feet in the soft drift. A few minutes later, they both stood panting, finally on a firm surface again.

"Nice job, pig," said Sophia between breaths. "Someone explain to me how hooves make sense at any time on any animal."

"I didn't hear you complaining when these hooves were kicking ship rats in the head so you could waltz up and bite them!" Flora hadn't meant to ever mention this matter, but now that her words were out, she was surprised at her strong feelings.

"Good point," Sophia said at last. "I'm not very good at saying sorry, but I apologize."

Flora didn't know how to respond, so she was happy when Sophia simply walked back onto the tracks.

The snow on this plain was different from any snow Flora had seen before. In fact, it wasn't really snow. Flora stepped out, and the ground crackled. She bent her head and looked closer. The field was covered with ice crystals sticking up like a garden of little diamonds. Sophia was beside her now, and the two animals walked slowly into the crystal blossoms. Flora was enchanted.

For a moment she forgot she was hungry, tired, and ill-equipped to make this journey. She forgot to worry about Oscar. She forgot to worry that there would never be a useful job for her. She kicked up her front hooves with each step and watched the ice crystals scatter in front of her.

But Sophia fell behind, picking her way along the trail tenderly.

When Flora looked back to see what was the matter, she saw a spot of red inside each of her friend's small footprints.

"Sophia," said Flora. "You're bleeding."

Sophia stopped. "Thanks for the info, Doc." She

227

licked her front paws, took another step and winced, but kept moving. "It's like walking on needles."

"Sophia, I think we just discovered one good use for hooves. Climb on my back."

"Impossible." Sophia swished her tail. "Does Sophia look like a circus monkey to you? Cats don't ride pigs. They don't ride anything if they have any dignity—and I'm saving my last shred."

"Who's going to laugh at you out here in the middle of nowhere?"

"I don't care. Sophia is no monkey, and you're no pony. Thank you."

Flora planted herself in front of Sophia. "I know cats like to be independent and everything," she said, "but you're going to hurt your paws, and then I'll really have to take care of you."

The tip of Sophia's tail twitched back and forth. "I suppose. But if you say a word of this to anyone . . ."

"I won't. I promise."

Sophia leaped easily onto Flora's broad back.

Flora looked out at the two smooth lines of sled tracks. They seemed to go on forever. But the sun was shining, and the trail ahead was clear. Her spirits lifted. She took her first few steps—

"Hey, watch the claws, Sheriff," Flora said. "You're digging them right through the coat and into my skin."

"Well, then, don't walk so bumpy!" snapped Sophia.

Flora slowed down and tried to smooth out her walk. "I wonder how Oscar was able to keep going in this stuff."

"Dog booties. Aleric was sewing some out of leather the night before they left. I think he got the idea from the sailors. All the other dogs had them."

The tracks in front of them led out in a straight line that went on for hours. Finally the ice crystals gave way to snow that became deeper and more and more powdery. Sophia hopped down and walked lightly across the surface. The churned-up snow between the sled tracks showed that Oscar and Aleric had to work hard to keep moving forward through the powder.

Flora also found the going tough, even after the land flattened out. Her hooves sank down until her jacket was dragging in the snow. She could no longer walk. Instead, she had to leap forward, charging through it. Every third leap she had to stop and catch her breath.

Sophia studied her. "I don't think this is working."

"Just go ahead," Flora panted. "You can go faster without me. When you catch up with them, let them know I'm coming."

Sophia paused for a moment and then without a word pranced away.

Flora watched until she disappeared, then tried to struggle on, but there was no more leap in her. All she could do was flounder in the right direction. She got more and more exhausted, and, each time she stopped, she imagined Sophia getting farther and farther ahead.

She began to talk to herself to find strength.

"Never . . . out . . . of . . . options."

With each stroke of her legs, Flora repeated the words Luna had taught her so long ago. Then she added a phrase. "Cats may have nine lives, but pigs . . . don't . . . give . . . up."

She worked like this until the light began to fade. Finally, Flora had to get some rest.

A cave was easy to make here. All she had to do was flop down and wiggle her body about. As she rested her head, she felt the soft feathers of fresh snowflakes land on her snout. Flora thought for a moment that a snowfall might be bad news, but she was too tired to be concerned.

Chapter 33

The next morning, Flora had to push her way through a heavy blanket of fresh snow. She shook it off and tried to ignore her grumbling stomach. To her surprise, Sophia was sitting a short ways off. She didn't turn around when Flora called her name, so Flora asked, "What's for breakfast?"

Sophia still didn't answer. Her tail swished a half circle in the snow.

Flora looked around in every direction.

A cold, hard lump grew in her throat.

"Sophia." Flora tried to swallow and couldn't. Her voice shook. "Where are the sled tracks? Where are our tracks?"

"Gone," said Sophia. "Covered over last night."

Flora looked out again, unbelieving. All of her

deep floundering from the day before had been completely cleaned up. The land was spotless and smooth. Flora felt like a tiny dot—she and Sophia, the only two things alive on the face of the earth.

Sophia stepped daintily up to Flora, shaking the snow from her paws.

"Why did you come back?" asked Flora.

"I'm sticking with my team." Sophia sat and looked down. "I know I said sorry yesterday, but I . . . um . . . never properly said thank you for helping me with those rats."

"How do you know I wasn't trying to get in good with Big Amos?" Flora asked.

"You kept helping me even after he chained you up again." Sophia looked long and hard into Flora's eyes.

Flora had never been able to stare back at a cat for long, even when it was a friendly stare from Luna. But this time it was the cat that looked away eventually.

"I've been corrupted," Sophia said. "I used to

have unfailing cat common sense. I hardly recognize myself anymore. What kind of cat takes up with dogs and pigs? But I can't help it. I'm a team member now, so I came back."

Flora smiled. "We need a plan."

"No plan is going to get us out of this mess." Sophia sounded as tired and hungry as Flora felt. "We're doomed. If Oscar doesn't come back the exact same way he went, we're finished."

Flora nudged Sophia with her nose. "Cats are good at keeping clean," she said. "Dogs are good at running forever without getting tired. And I think that pigs are good at being optimistic and not giving up even when things are really bad. So today we're going to do things the pig way, okay?"

Flora explained her idea. She and Sophia would walk in a straight line away from each other until the middle of the day. Then they'd turn around, follow their paths back, and meet in the middle again. This way, Oscar and Aleric were sure to come across the tracks on their return trip.

Flora began to walk. It was no easier than before. She knew that she would go more slowly through the deep snow than her lighter friend, but she also knew that her tracks would be deeper and easier for Oscar to recognize.

When Flora turned around at midday, her heart lifted as she headed toward Sophia. She still couldn't believe that crazy cat had come back in the night to find her. If Sophia had followed the sled tracks before they disappeared, she might have located Oscar and Aleric, which would have meant finding food and rescue. She'd had the chance to save herself. It wasn't in her nature to make a decision for the sake of a friend. But that was what it seemed she had done.

At the end of the day, Flora and Sophia met in the middle again. When Flora saw how tired Sophia was, instead of throwing her tired body down as she wanted to, Flora slowly dug out a fresh snow cave. She and Sophia collapsed together without a word. For that, Flora was thankful. She didn't want to have to hide her disappointment. She had silently hoped that Aleric and Oscar would have shown up by now.

Flora closed her eyes and had one happy thought. So far, there didn't appear to be any wind or snowfall tonight to undo their hard work.

Chapter 34

The next morning it wasn't the cold or the hunger pangs that woke Flora. It wasn't a soft meow or the delicious smell of food in her dreams.

It was a big sloppy lick from a big sloppy tongue!

"Oscar!" Flora squealed, and jumped up in a spray of powder.

Sophia yowled in surprise at being woken this way, but she soon joined Flora in dancing around their friend.

Aleric stood smiling a short way off. He was still hooked to the sled, while Oscar's line lay in the snow.

"I knew you would find us!" shouted Flora. "I knew you'd come back the same way you went."

Oscar's wagging tail flew up. "What are you two doing out here?"

"Looking for you." Sophia ran with her tail high to Aleric and climbed his legs until she was in his arms. Aleric laughed.

"We were afraid you wouldn't be strong enough to make it." Flora bumped Oscar's chin with her nose and got another lick in return.

"You don't know how tough an old dog can be," said Oscar. But Flora thought he looked rundown— exhausted even.

"We wanted to help you get the food, but we lost your tracks," said Flora.

"Well, it's a good thing you left some tracks yourself, because otherwise we would have passed you right by. We started back only today, and the sled is a lot heavier."

Flora held her breath for a moment. "You found the food?" She looked over at the sled, and her mouth began watering.

Aleric had unwrapped the load and was giving Sophia something. Then he waded through the deep snow to deliver two frozen fish to Flora.

Those two fish were the sweetest things she could ever remember tasting. Aleric stayed close while she ate and, when she was done, bent down and hugged her. "You are one crazy pig, you know that? You disappear and then show up at the wildest times. What are you doing out here?"

Aleric walked back to the sled, tossed Flora two more fish, and then whistled. Oscar trudged his way to his pull line. Aleric hooked him to his harness, and they started out, the boy and dog side by side and the sled behind with Sophia on top.

They could only creep.

Flora watched for another moment and then plowed through the snow until she was out in front of Oscar. The food had revived her, and she was determined to be helpful. She was going to make a path for him. She knew getting through the deep powder would be even harder for Oscar with the heavy load. Every step she took packed the snow down and made it easier for her friend. Knowing this made the work easier for her, too.

But being homemade, the sled didn't slide as smoothly as it should have. Sometimes Aleric

stashed his pull line on the food box and dropped behind to push.

When they finally passed the stretch of deep

drifts and were back on more solid snow, the company stopped for a breather. Flora made her way to where Sophia had hopped down and was watching over Oscar. He hadn't bothered to wait for Aleric to take off the rope before collapsing.

Flora was alarmed to hear the rattling in his throat again. "Oscar, you don't sound so good," she said. He didn't answer. He was too busy trying to catch his breath.

Aleric knelt by the dog's side. "Here you go, boy. Let's get that line off you." He unfastened the rope and rubbed Oscar's side for a few minutes. Then he went to check on the food boxes.

"Pulling . . . is like . . . medicine," panted Oscar.

"I think you might be getting a little too much medicine on this trip," said Sophia. "Can't you take it easier?"

Oscar didn't say more, and all too soon Aleric came back to hook him up. The dog struggled to his feet. Before long they came to the field of ice crystals. Flora hadn't noticed the leather booties on Oscar's feet until now, but there they were, just as Sophia had said.

The icy crust that supported the crystals was thick enough to hold Flora and Oscar's weight. But the much heavier sled kept breaking through, causing the runners to end up stuck in the soft snow underneath. When this happened, Aleric had to yank the sled back through the crust and find a new path.

They would travel only a short distance before the sled would break through again. There was nothing Flora could do to help.

Finally, Aleric leaned against the sled. "Night's coming, anyway." Stumbling forward, he unhooked Oscar, who just lay on the snow with his sides heaving. Aleric brought out a tent and a small stove. Soon supper was cooking, and Flora could almost taste the warm fish stew.

It might have been a happy time, Flora thought.

They were rescuers coming back to save the day. They had enough to eat. But there was no cheer in the small camp.

Flora and Sophia stayed near Oscar, who didn't move from where he had dropped. When supper was ready, he wouldn't eat. His throat was still rattling.

"Come on, boy. I'm depending on you," Aleric coaxed. "You're my engine. I didn't work you too hard, did I?"

When it was time to sleep, Aleric carried him inside the tent. Flora poked her head through the opening. The boy had made a bed of blankets for Oscar next to his own bed. "You'll feel better tomorrow, buddy," he said.

Sophia stepped into the tent and curled up at the dog's side. Aleric crawled inside his blankets and patted the space on the other side of him. "Come on, pig. There's room for everyone, and this tent needs all the body heat it can get."

Flora lay beside Aleric, thinking about the captain. How was he doing without the body heat of a pig to warm him? Then she listened to the rough sound of Oscar's breathing a long time before she went to sleep.

Chapter 35

In the morning, Flora was the first one outside. This was going to be a hard day. She might as well have a moment to herself while she could.

The new sky showed points of light—stars that weren't ready to leave their place yet. Like little eyes, they were watching and blinking from high above the world. She thought of the stars looking down on her mother and brothers and Luna on the farm, and she wondered how two such different places could exist in the same world.

If she ever went back, what stories she'd have to tell. Rat hunting. Captain rescuing. And now . . .

She pawed listlessly at the snow around the sled runners. Her coat felt like a second skin, and she was warm. But nothing could warm up her thoughts, which had turned chilly.

No way could Oscar pull that sled for another day, even with Aleric helping. The problem was, Oscar would try. There was no quit in that dog and he would pull and pull . . . until he died. If Oscar didn't make it back to camp, if this little trip failed, it wouldn't be a disaster for them alone. Flora blinked.

Was the captain wondering why they had deserted him?

Maybe the sailor's leg would get better and he'd hobble out to look for them. Maybe he'd stumble over their frozen bodies. Then at least the captain would know they'd been trying to help.

"See?" the sailor would say. "They reached the supplies. Just didn't have a sled dog strong enough to get them to us."

Sled puller, she corrected him in her mind.

Flora grunted. Her snout tingled. She looked up again at the stars.

Where were all these terrible thoughts coming from?

She walked away from the sled and stared back at it for a long time. Flora couldn't change the cold or the snow or whether someone thought of her as food. But she could believe in herself again—just as she used to.

By the time the others were ready to go, Flora was in place. Oscar dragged himself out of the tent, looking as if the night's sleep had not helped much. He glanced around, confused when he couldn't see his harness on the snow. He wandered over and sniffed Aleric's empty line before seeming to wake up to what was going on.

Oscar got in Flora's face and growled. "This is not a job for pigs! We're not playing now—we're working here!"

When Flora didn't move, he snarled and snapped at her.

Flora stepped sideways. This was not good. She

wasn't going to be a very strong sled puller with teeth marks in her snout. She quickly slipped out of the harness and hurried to the back of the sled.

Aleric packed the tent, pots, and other equipment, then hooked himself and Oscar up to pull. The going was easier today. The crust of ice on the surface of the snow had firmed up in the night. The sled runners ran more smoothly, but Oscar still stumbled at times.

Aleric was on one side of him, pulling, and Flora walked along on the other side—but a little bit behind, so she didn't have to face Oscar's anger again.

She was glad to see Aleric change course to go around the hill they had slid down. On this new path, the ice crystals ended and the land gradually sloped upward. After a few minutes, the snow softened again and the sled got stuck in a small snowdrift. Aleric slipped out of his loop and went to push.

Flora didn't hesitate.

She ran and nosed Aleric's loop of rope around

her neck. "You'll just have to bite me," she said to Oscar.

He lifted his lips to show his teeth, but he was breathing so hard, he couldn't do much more.

When the sled was freed, Aleric walked to the front. He laughed. "Ho, piggy. You're a funny one. Listen here—pigs don't pull." He took the loop off Flora and put it around his own shoulders. "You just be sure to make it safely back to the captain, because he would never forgive me if something happened to the pig that saved his life."

Flora wished she could talk in a way that Aleric understood. Instead, she walked patiently behind the sled, and when it got stuck again, she walked to the front, as Aleric went back to push, and slipped into the loop.

Oscar's sides were heaving. His legs trembled, and he made no move to stop her.

This time, when she felt Aleric pushing, she pulled with all her might. Her hooves dug in, and the sled jerked forward.

Sophia yowled in surprise.

"Whoa!" called Aleric.

Flora looked back but didn't stop. Sophia was standing up to her stomach in soft snow where she had jumped off the sled, and Aleric was on his hands and knees, not expecting the sled to move so quickly.

Flora faced forward. *Step. Step. Pull. Pull. Pigs . . . don't . . . give . . . up.*

Aleric came running. "Whoa, whoa, whoa!" He pulled back on the rope until the sled stopped. Then he knelt down and scratched Flora behind the ears. "This can't be happening. You're really pulling the sled—you and Oscar."

He took the rope off Flora's neck, and she was afraid he was going to tell her to go away. But instead he adjusted the loop, making it the right size for her. Then he rummaged in one of the food boxes until he came up with a soft cloth that he placed around the loop so that the rope wouldn't bite into her skin above her coat.

"There we go, then, pig." He patted her on the shoulder. "I guess the captain was right—it's hard to know where brains and talent are going to come from. Let's see if this can really work."

Flora pulled all day. It was hard, but the sled no longer got stuck. She had little idea where she was going. But Oscar obviously knew. Even though he couldn't pull very hard, he would growl and tug in certain directions to correct their course or snap at her shoulder to push her the other way.

Sophia ran up now and then to encourage Flora, but most of the time the cat stayed on the other side, keeping Oscar's spirits up.

Flora was sad to see it wasn't working. The dog's head drooped further and further. His rope often went slack for long periods while he walked and heaved. Flora was afraid to talk to him, so she just kept pulling.

They stopped at the end of the day close to the giant chunks of ice that Flora remembered from their trip out. She barely had enough energy to eat before crawling into the tent to sleep. Her tired muscles ached. Her shoulders were sore where she had pulled against the rope. But she felt a glow of pride deep in her bones.

Sophia curled up next to Flora's cheek and whispered, "You were amazing. We could never have made it without you."

A little while later, Aleric came in carrying Oscar. He laid him down, crawled into his blanket, and blew out the candle. All was quiet when the dog got up and stumbled back outside.

"Where's Oscar going?" whispered Flora.

"I guess he wants to sleep outside tonight," Sophia mumbled.

Flora listened for his breathing or some sound that would tell her he was lying in the snow close by. There was nothing. Finally she dragged her aching body out of the warmth and into the night. Sophia didn't stir.

The sled looked ready for their final push tomorrow. But Oscar was nowhere to be seen. Flora walked around the camp until she found what she was looking for.

A trail of dog prints led out into the white emptiness.

Flora swallowed hard—and then followed them. She didn't hurry. She wasn't worried about being able to catch Oscar. But she wasn't looking forward to facing him. She didn't know what he would do when he saw her.

Eventually, she spotted a dark shape in the moonlight.

Oscar turned his head when he heard her behind him. Flora quieted her heart. She was determined not to leave without him and prepared to fight back even if she had to face his teeth.

"Leave me alone," he snarled when she walked up.

"Where are you going?"

"It doesn't matter." Oscar set out again. His tail dragged in the snow.

Flora kept in step beside him. She gathered her courage. "We need you back there."

"You're lying!" Oscar lunged at her and snapped his teeth next to her cheek.

Flora flinched, but she didn't back away.

Oscar growled into her ear, "I don't deserve to be called a sled dog any longer. It's over for me."

Oscar picked up the pace. Flora followed.

"Go back." He didn't turn to look at her. "You're the only one now who can pull that sled to the main camp."

"I've wanted to be a sled pig for a long time,"

Flora said. "I've put in a lot of practice, and I'm glad I got the chance to prove myself. But it won't do any good, because I can't find my way home."

"It's easy," Oscar answered. "You'll be fine."

"Easy for you. I get all confused in this snow. I can't even walk in a straight line without getting turned around."

"You're just making excuses, pig. Aleric can find his way. He's a smart kid." Oscar kept walking. "I'm finished."

Flora stepped in front and stopped him. She stared at him until he looked her in the eyes. "You're not finished. You're sick. You're tired. You're overworked. You're not as young as you used to be, but you're not finished."

Oscar sank into the snow. "I was born and bred to be a sled dog. It's all I've ever known. It's all I was ever good for. And now I can't outpull a pig."

Flora took a deep breath. "At least you were born and bred to have a job. You know what I was born and bred for. Now I have a chance to live and to be really useful. But it doesn't matter, because I can't find my way, and you won't help me. Where's your team spirit?"

"My team left without me because I wasn't strong enough!" Oscar snapped.

"You have a new team now," said Flora. "We won't leave without you. I won't. Sophia won't. Aleric won't."

Oscar blinked, and Flora recalled the first time she had seen him so long ago on the farm. It felt strange to be reminding a sled dog about team spirit, and it made her notice how different she was from the pig that left the farm in the back of a truck.

"Oscar, you're a dog, and your first instincts will always be doglike. But in another way, you're not like other dogs." Flora stopped and watched his face, but she was thinking about her next words. She wanted to say it just right.

"You're more than a dog, and I know this because of the way you've always looked out for me. Sophia's a cat, but she has been changing. I didn't tell you that she came back for me when I couldn't go on."

Flora lay down at Oscar's side. "And then there's me, and I'm pretty sure you've noticed that I try hard not to be too piglike. I think we're all aiming to be something better than what everyone thinks we were born to be, and that makes us even more of a team. We have to stick together."

Oscar had put his head on his paws. He wasn't moving. He wasn't even breathing, and his eyes had a glassy look.

"Oscar?" said Flora softly—and a chill suddenly went through her. "Oscar!" she shrieked, and jumped to her feet.

Oscar picked up his head and looked at her. "I'm right here. Why are you screaming?"

"Oh, Oscar, I thought you were . . . gone," Flora choked out. "Like, gone forever."

"I'm not dead, you nut." Oscar got to his feet and began to walk toward camp. "Come on. Let's get back to the others and get some sleep. It's going to be a long day tomorrow."

"You changed your mind?" Flora could hardly believe it. She trotted up beside him.

"Yes, and I'll change it again if you keep yakking. I've heard enough for one night," he muttered. "Cat but not a cat. Pig but not a pig." He snorted. "Dog but not a dog."

"*More* than a dog," Flora corrected.

They walked in silence until the tent came into view. Then Oscar stopped. "About this business of pulling sleds, listen up."

Flora stopped too. Was he going to start fighting again?

"You're doing it wrong, and you're going to wear yourself out."

Flora hadn't noticed she was holding her breath, but she let it out now.

Oscar continued. "Keep your head down when you're pulling. You're not a goat or a fancy pony. That's rule number two. Rule number one: If you want to be a good sled dog . . . I mean puller . . . you gotta get your sleep. I'll teach you rules three through sixty-six tomorrow."

"Yes, sir!" Flora answered.

They walked in silence again. Flora felt nervous, but she had to know something.

"I understand that I need my sleep, but can I ask just one question?"

"Rule number one: Nothing is more important than sleep."

"Right. But I have a question that may be important."

"Okay, what?"

"When we first met, you said that sled dogs go a little crazy. Does that happen at the end of the journey?"

Oscar stopped walking. "I didn't say they go a little crazy. I said they have to *be* a little crazy to work this hard and enjoy it."

"Oh." Flora looked at Oscar. "Because I thought you meant they do a crazy little dance or something."

259

Oscar stared at her as if a horn had suddenly sprouted from her forehead.

"Kind of a shimmy with some high-stepping at the end?" Flora summoned some energy and high-stepped her tired body across the snow to demonstrate.

Oscar shook his head as he started walking again. "I don't know anything about that."

"What about a dance at the end to celebrate . . ."

"Sled dogs don't dance."

"I'm a sled *pig*," Flora whispered. They were back at camp now, and she didn't want to wake the others. "It might be different for me."

Oscar sighed. "You just get up tomorrow ready to pull." He nosed into the tent.

Flora looked up. The stars were extra bright tonight, and they shone and glimmered as if each one had something it wanted to say.

Oscar poked his head out. "You coming?"

Chapter 36

Oscar was so stiff the next morning, Aleric didn't even bother hooking him up.

"Take it easy for a while till you get better, boy," he said, and made a bed for the dog on top of the food boxes. "If I'd had any choice, I wouldn't have worked you so hard."

Flora placed herself at the front of the sled. She was sore, but she had slept well and could feel Oscar's confidence cover her like a warm blanket.

"I might as well make a harness for you today, pig," said Aleric. "It'll be easier on your neck."

She was thankful for this, especially when she saw Aleric struggling with the knots and blowing on his fingers to warm them up. When he was finished, the rope looped around her chest and between her front legs and up either side of her ribs. The whole arrangement fit over her coat, and once they were moving, helped make the pulling much easier.

"Hike!" shouted Aleric when everything was ready.

"Head down when you pull!" barked Oscar from his place on the sled. "Remember rule number two: Head down until you get up to speed. Let your shoulders do the work, not your neck."

Flora smiled, put her head down, and pulled.

"Rule number three: Pace yourself. Don't wear yourself out before you get where you're going."

Flora eased up a bit and turned her head. "I know someone who needs to practice that rule."

"Rule number four: Do not turn around while you're pulling. And rule number five: Do as I say, not as I do."

From time to time Oscar barked out directions, and Flora would steer left or right to keep on course. Aleric pulled from the front or rolled the rope up and pushed from the back.

Just before nightfall, Flora heard Sophia give out a loud yowl. "I think I see something! Hey, Deputy, look up ahead!"

Flora broke into a trot the camp came into view.

Aleric hollered.

Far ahead, Flora saw two specks come limping out of the snow shelter.

They'd done it!

No one was going to die—not now, anyway.

Excitement and happiness bubbled inside her, and then she couldn't help it. Tiredness and sore muscles dropped away as she reared up on her hind legs and hopped. She trotted a bit more and then kicked her back legs to one side, then the other. Behind her, Oscar started barking. "Dance and shimmy all you want, pig. You did it!"

Flora surged against the rope one last time. She jumped and twisted in a crazy little dance as the sled coasted in.

Chapter 37

Both the captain and the other sailor hobbled over to meet them and cheered. Aleric whooped some more. After a lot of shouting and smiling and back slapping, the food boxes were opened, and soon there was an aroma of soup made from something other than fish.

Over dinner, the captain wanted to know all about the trip. He didn't seem angry in the least. Flora stayed close by his side as Aleric told the story. All eyes were on her when Aleric got to the place where Flora insisted on putting her shoulder to the rope. At the end, Aleric started to apologize for leaving without permission, but the captain held up his hand.

"I would have done the very same thing. It wasn't my place to send a youngster out on a rescue mission alone. But it was courage and duty that made you ignore my order. And you'll be welcome on my ship anytime."

He reached down and scratched Flora between her ears.

Flora looked up, full of hope. Might she be welcome on his ship too?

Later that night, Flora checked in on Oscar. He was sound asleep on his bed. Someone had covered him with extra blankets, which he hadn't kicked off this time. Flora snuggled in with Sophia under their blanket, and if not for the glow in her heart, she might have wondered if the sled-pulling adventure was just a dream.

The next three weeks were spent resting up. With bellies full each day, everyone's spirits lifted. The sailor, who seemed completely recovered now, no longer looked at Flora with hungry eyes. The captain took a daily walk with a cane. He always called Flora to go with him.

Flora and Sophia kept a close eye on Oscar at first, but they didn't need to. Aleric made it his full-time job to look after the dog. The boy took him out of the shelter for fresh air two times a day but otherwise kept him inside and warm with extra blankets. When Oscar's appetite came back, Aleric slipped him an extra helping each day. Slowly the dog's health improved, and even the rattle in his throat disappeared.

One bright morning, it was time to say good-bye to the camp forever.

The two men loaded Aleric's sled with all the blankets and food. The captain admired the home-made harnesses as Aleric took care to properly adjust them both. Flora and Oscar were hooked up side by side at the front of the sled, and this time they were going to head in the direction the sailors had gone to find help.

"Remember what I told you." Oscar couldn't hide his excitement at being back in a harness again. He practically vibrated with energy.

"Let me see . . ." Flora pretended to be deep in thought. "Rule number one: Get enough sleep. Rule two: Pull with your shoulders and not your neck. Rule three: Remember that dogs have way too many rules."

Sophia laughed from where she was waiting on top of the load.

"Rule number sixty-six." Oscar grinned. "You can never have too many rules."

"Everyone ready?" the captain called. The two men and Aleric placed their hands on the sled to help push the heavy load. "Move out!"

Flora and Oscar put their shoulders into their harnesses and pulled. The sled resisted for a moment and then lurched forward as it broke away from where the runners had become frozen to the ice.

In all the excitement, Flora was surprised to feel a tightness in her heart. The camp was where she had found the courage to be more than just a farm pig, to take a little control of her life. She was tempted to turn for one last look, except she knew she'd hear the rule about not turning around again.

A little later, they passed by a spot Flora was certain she had seen before. Then she remembered. It was the place where Oscar had dug the hole for her to hide in. She imagined filling up that dark place with fresh white powder, and she promised herself she'd never lose hope like that again.

On the second day out, they met the rescue party coming toward them. People laughed and pointed when they saw who was pulling the sled, and then a huge cheer filled the air. Hugs were given, and Flora got her share. Even Amos tickled her ears. But it was clear from their pinched faces that the food in the boxes would be a welcome surprise.

Oscar and Flora were unhooked from their lines. Sniffing noses and wagging tails immediately surrounded Oscar. Flora felt awkward and out of place among the other dogs. But as soon as he could, Oscar told them the story of their adventure, giving full credit to Flora and her pulling skills. Each dog came up to thank her personally, which meant Flora got plenty of practice touching noses, apparently a requirement in the dog world.

Even Sophia felt safe enough to jump down and wander through the furry crowd, though she wanted nothing to do with the sniffing and gave any dog that tried it a sharp smack on the snout.

After a warm meal had been cooked up, eaten, and cleared away, coils of rope were brought out and more lines were tied to the sled. Flora was proud to be placed back in her harness even though there was far too much laughter over it from the other men. She was gratified that none of the dogs seemed to think it was funny. They waited patiently to be hooked up.

"Hike!" shouted the captain from his place on the sled.

Flora threw herself forward at the signal, and the men standing nearby cheered. Two of them ran alongside for a few steps, waving their hats. "Go, pig! Pull, pig!"

Pulling with a full team was not only a wonderful feeling, it was a lot easier than what she was used to. In just three days they reached the sea and the camp where they hoped to be saved. From here, a group of the strongest sailors had set sail in the lifeboat to intercept a ship or find the nearest settlement on the southern tip of South America.

If they were successful, rescuers could arrive any day now.

Chapter 38

The day the large ship appeared, the men hugged one another and danced while the dogs barked. As it sailed closer, Flora could see it was painted as white as snow. She watched with the others until she could make out its name written in tall red letters, the *Undefeated*. It dropped anchor, and a lifeboat was lowered into the water.

As soon as the men in the boat stepped onto the ice, there was another round of hugging among comrades.

The captain still walked with a cane, but he was in charge again as he called out orders and directed the action. The lifeboat began taking men and dogs to the ship.

Flora's feelings were all jumbled and confused.

She wasn't sure what to think now that they were rescued. She wasn't sure she should be celebrating like the men and dogs around her. Her future seemed uncertain.

She turned to find a friend and almost stumbled over Sophia, who was also not celebrating. Flora found it hard to push the words over the lump in her throat. "What happens now?"

Sophia didn't answer at first. "We animals don't get to decide, at least not usually," she said, and almost smiled. "Well, anyway, we're back to depending on the kindness of people and trusting they get it right. Hopefully Aleric and the captain will remember us once all of this excitement dies down."

Flora took a deep breath. "Remind me to tell you about a cat friend I had when I was a piglet who always said that nine lives were a state of mind. Whatever happens will be an adventure, right?"

"That's for sure." Sophia licked her whiskers. "Whatever happens, I'm sticking with you."

Oscar walked up. He seemed relaxed and confident. "You two ready to go?"

Flora didn't know what to say, and Sophia just stared straight ahead, her tail sweeping slowly back and forth on the snow.

"Come on, guys. Don't worry. I heard the captain giving a couple of special orders," said Oscar. "I think you're going to feel at home on this ship."

"Do they have a rat problem?" Flora asked hopefully.

"All ships have a rat problem," said Oscar, "but that's not what I'm talking about."

"Then what do you mean?" asked Flora.

"Rule number one hundred: Let your friends figure things out for themselves sometimes. You'll see."

Just then, Aleric came over, picked up Sophia, and motioned for Flora to follow. He guided them toward the boat, calling for Oscar.

"Come on, everyone. No one gets left behind this time," he said.

Sophia hopped into the lifeboat first. Then Aleric

helped Flora and Oscar climb aboard. In a few moments, the *Undefeated*'s bright white sides towered above the small craft. A large box was lowered down with ropes. Oscar was lifted into the box, which was hauled upward until Flora couldn't see him any longer. The box came down again.

"Your turn, pig," said Aleric.

Flora put her front hooves on the side of the box, and Aleric lifted her in. Sophia hopped in beside her.

Up and up went the box in a jerky, unsteady motion. Flora spread out her feet as far as possible to keep from falling. Sophia jumped onto the ship as soon as she could. Strong hands helped Flora onto the deck, and she looked around.

This was a step up from the *Explorer*!

The *Undefeated* was bigger and newer, and it smelled of fresh paint. Even the sailors' shouts and the pounding of their boots were louder to Flora's ears. After all that time in the soft snow, it felt strange to be walking on a smooth surface again.

Flora looked around for the door that led to the ship's hold. But Oscar walked up and steered them, instead, to the front of the ship.

They passed rows of sturdy sled-dog crates with new, soft blankets inside. Flora felt the old pang of jealousy return. She took a breath and lifted her face to the pale blue sky above. A few delicate white clouds were spread out above the horizon.

Flora suddenly regretted that she hadn't taken more time to notice the sky during her time on land. The hold was going to be awfully dark. Right now the sky seemed the most beautiful thing she had ever seen. She tried to capture it in her mind for later . . .

Bang! A sailor clomped by, and Flora jumped.

"Pick up the pace or get out of the way!" Oscar called.

"Come on, Flora," Sophia said.

Flora trotted up to her friends. The very first two crates had been given a new coat of light blue paint. Over the door of one, a sign read LEAD DOG.

"That's my home right there," said Oscar.

Good for Oscar. He deserved it.

Oscar walked over to the other one and looked up at the sign. " 'The Captain's Gratitude,' " he read. "This one is for the two of you."

It couldn't be!

"How—how do you . . . Are you sure?" Flora asked.

"Captain's first order," said Oscar. "I heard him say to get these boxes painted and lettered."

Flora felt a sea breeze flutter her ears. "What does *gratitude* mean?"

"I'm not sure. Maybe it's about paying back a favor," answered Oscar. "Or maybe it just means 'the best pig ever.' " He gave her a big doggy grin.

The ship's whistle blew again. Sophia and Flora looked at each other. "Think you can handle being a ship's best pig?" asked Sophia.

"Hmm," said Flora. "Let me think about this . . . Travel all over the world? Hunt rats and pull sleds? Wake up next to your best friends? New adventure every trip?"

"Tough duty, huh?" asked Oscar.

"I'll just have to make the best of it," said Flora. "Starting now."

As the ship picked up speed, Flora walked to the tip of the bow and put her feet on the railing, facing the wind—and all her adventures to come.